WIND

WITHOUT

RAIN

WIND
WITHOUT
RAIN

James Hallaux

Calvin Cahail

ISBN: 9781092201711

Acknowledgments

This book is dedicated to our wives, Mariana, and Robbie. For putting up with us through the writing of this book and everything else.

Calvin Cahail

Jim Hallaux

The authors wish to thank the following for allowing us in their establishments for inordinate periods of time with computers, notes, glasses, and coffee cups spread across tables, bars, and counters;

Columbia House, Workers Tavern, 3 Cups Coffee, Coffee Girl, Taps, Zipline Café, Blue Scorcher, Ship Out, Portway Tavern, Golden Star.

Cast of Characters

The Lovers

     Merri Sue Morrison

     Thomas Thompson

The People's Army

     Peter Aro

     Bill Nikula

     Joe Lagerstrom

     Mr. X – Andre Demico

The Job Corps

     Penny, Best Friend

     Sally, Good Looking Trouble

     Sammi, Roommate

     Larry Alred, Counselor

Like clouds and wind without rain is a man who boasts of a gift he does not give.
Proverbs 25:14

PART ONE
Wind Without Rain

1

1969

MERRI SUE HAD TWO STRONG EARLY MEMORIES; one a scent and the other a sound.

The scent was juniper, creosote, and sage. Early on summer mornings, before the day turned hot, with the window open to let in fresh air, the smell drifted into Merri's room. If she could only bottle that wonderful aroma of the high Eastern Oregon desert.

The sound ate at her stomach. Her parents arguing like summer thunderstorms. Quick to start. Angry, harsh words that Merri heard in her room behind the closed door not understanding. Two memories that haunted Merri's life.

Merri's father held a temper lurking under the surface. He was a man of average height and above average strength. As a small child Merri adored her father. Later she feared him and then hated him. But always, she loved him and always he let her down.

Her father taught Merri how to ride a bike, how to fish, how to ride a horse. She cherished those times with her father. Between these, she experienced any number of violent outbursts. It was always something Mom did or didn't do. The worst times were when he had been drinking. The temper simmered like a low flame. The alcohol like kerosene. At first, words; demeaning, obscene, hurtful words. The violence came later. Merri hid in her room and waited, praying it would end soon. And sometimes it did. Her father promised her it would not happen again, but it always did. The waiting made it worse.

Merri, only a child, saw and heard all of this on her own. She had friends, but Merri always went to their houses to play, never at her house. Reaching high school, Merri never had dates pick her up at the house, she always met them somewhere else. She didn't date much; it was just too hard and complicated. Merri immersed herself in school and stayed in her room at home. They were her haven and her prison. Later in life, her grocery store and drive-in jobs were havens.

After graduation, with college being out of the question, Merri did both jobs. She became the major breadwinner for the family. Often, her mother showed up at her hardware store job with swollen eyes and bruises. The store cut her hours so low that it didn't make sense for her to go in.

Merri and her Mother had the same talk again and again. It went from a talk to an argument to a shouting match. Always the same.

"Mom, he will kill you. If we don't get out now, it will happen. Dad will get drunk, he'll hit you too hard, he doesn't realize how strong he is when he drinks, how mad he gets. He'll knock you down; hit your head. However, it happens, on purpose or by accident, he'll kill you just the same."

"You don't understand, child. He gets mad sometimes and loses his temper and does and says things he doesn't mean. I can take care of myself. Your Dad loves me. You worry about your life. I can take care of myself."

"You are my life. This is my life. The yelling, the hitting, waiting for the next time. All of it. This is my life and I hate it."

"Child, child, he loves me. You'll see. It will get better."

But it didn't.

During this time, Merri did have a boyfriend. Ted was as different from her dad as he could be. He was kind, funny, and slow to anger. Merri loved that the most. She always felt safe with Ted. She did not introduce him to her parents though. He never picked her up at home.

The romance started in the summer and by fall was serious. Merri was the most hopeful she had ever been. A new love, a new life, a way out. When Merri missed her period, it was the first serious problem they had faced.

"We need to decide what to do," she told him.

"We need to get married. They said at the gas station I'm getting a raise. I can get a second job. We will work this out. I love you." Those were Ted's promises.

After not hearing from Ted for a couple of days, Merri called him.

"I'm thinking about what we should do," he said. "Gonna go on a hunting trip south with the boys. I need time to think."

Merri's period came the day after Ted left. When he came back, he took another trip. This one to Reno with the boys. More time to think. When he got back, Merri didn't care. The summer romance didn't last through the fall.

Her father had too many jobs to count. Fired for showing up late, drunk, or not showing up at all. Sometimes arguments and fights with coworkers; sometimes with bosses. Her father always said that the next job would be the one, but it never came to be. And the abuse and violence came more and more often.

Merri came home from work at the grocery. Her mother made scrambled eggs and bacon for her dinner before she left for work at the drive-in. Merri was in her room, changing into her drive-in uniform when she heard the slap and a sickening thud.

"Listen, you bitch…" and everything changed. Merri didn't need to know what he said next. She bounded to the kitchen. Her father, drunk, stood over her mother in front of the stove. Her mother slumped forward, head hung low, hands resting on her knees, trying to stand, leaning hard against the refrigerator.

Merri grabbed the hot cast-iron frying pan ignoring the heat of the handle searing her palm. She felt the pan connect with her father's head; indent the skull, high on his forehead. As he went down, she hit him again, harder, on the back of his head. He was on the floor now. Smaller. Diminished.

Blood pooled around him.

"Mom, we need to go now."

"I can't, Merri." She looked into Merri's eyes, torn. "You know I can't."

"Mom, he's never going to change. Can't you see that?"

"He just needs to find a job. Get settled again. Things'll get better. He's promised me."

"And that's gotten you where Mom?" Merri touched a compassionate hand to her mom's face. "I have to go."

Merri had heard the same argument many times. But this was the last time.

Merri took her cardboard suitcase out of the closet, threw in clothes without much thought, and grabbed the money she had stashed in a cigar box under her bed. She put her jacket on and headed for the front door.

"I'm leaving now."

Her mother knelt over her father trying to stop the blood with a dishrag, her hands drenched in blood.

Merri was at the door.

"Wait, Merri."

Merri's mother didn't say more. Crying by her husband.

Merri looked back through the cracked front window where no curtains hung. She stared at her mother for a long moment. Her mother made her decision and Merri Sue made hers.

2

A JUNIOR HIGH SCHOOL COUNSELOR in Astoria referred to Tom as a 'high functioning screw up.' His parents, a grade school teacher, and a high school vice principal, were shocked to hear this description of their only son and said so. But they secretly believed it.

It wasn't that people didn't like Tom or that he wasn't bright enough. It was just that given a choice of three paths; the right way, the easy way, or the absolutely, positively wrong way; Tom always started in the middle and inevitably worked his way to the wrong.

In grade school it had been taunting girls; the occasional black eye was given & received; the many timeouts at home and at school. From there it got worse. Each year, Tom's grades, not great to begin with, continued to go south. Tom wasn't just 'not living up to his ability'; he didn't even try. By high school, which he attended sporadically, his parents became desperate. Still loved him, but everything they tried failed.

About this time, alcohol and drugs came into play. Tom didn't like school, hated sports, and wasn't much interested in girls and not much interest was shown to him by girls. Drugs and liquor; that was something Tom could get behind in a big way.

He started to hang with a 'bad crowd.' Not a terribly bright or ambitious crowd, but interested in drugs and booze, the same two things Tom was interested in. Getting drugs wasn't so hard, but getting booze seemed to always be a hassle. Sometimes they could find an adult to buy the booze, prompted either by money or an invitation to share. Other times they would steal their parent's liquor, drink half, then fill it back to the top with water and replace the bottle in the liquor cabinet. Surprisingly, this worked.

But then Tom's crew decided to stop with the small-time scores and go straight to the source, the Oregon State Liquor Store on Duane Street in Astoria.

This was to be Tom's first brush with serious crime, although that wasn't really considered. It was just a natural extension of the path he was on. His school pals, Bill & Pete, were on board for this hastily conceived plan.

It wasn't exactly 'breaking & entering' because there was no entering. Tom and his two friends, armed with a claw hammer and a large rubber mallet, could not conquer the metal clad door but did pound on it long enough to trigger the silent alarm. This brought the police, who found three youths, two of them running away. The one that remained, his arms dead tired, ears ringing; appeared to be waiting to be arrested. A night in city lockup took the fun out of the enterprise.

Now things got very serious, very fast. Tom's parents had had enough. The wrecked car, the three speeding tickets, expulsions from grade school, junior & senior high schools, a rarely achieved trifecta. It was all too much.

A hasty meeting with a friendly Astoria judge was quietly arranged. The judge was a family friend who had known Tom since birth and was now seriously concerned and seriously pissed at him. He chose his words carefully.

"Tom, you have three choices; keep doing what you're doing, and I'll be seeing you again real soon. First, I'll be sending you for another stay in the city lockup. Then you'll graduate to the county jail and then for sure on to State prison. Think of it as dumb, dumber and then just plain stupid."

"On the other hand, there is a new federal program, called the Job Corps here in Astoria. Right now, they are mostly accepting young adults from the South, but I believe with my good recommendation we might get you in. They just started at Tongue Point; in fact, this is only the second Job Corps site in the nation. It is exactly what a person like you needs," said the judge. He ticked off the benefits on his fingers. "A kick in the butt, a direction in how to behave like a serious person, a high school diploma, a trade, and a job when you get out. All of this in a year and a half.

"Another way is the Marine Corp. The Corp is not at all interested in a serious screw-up or in bright people doing stupid things. So, it would be tough to get you in but maybe, just maybe, I could pull some strings.

"Just remember that in the Corp the penalty for screwing up is immediate and pretty damn harsh."

Tom chose the Job Corps.

3

EVEN AFTER LIVING FOR 20 YEARS in this small eastern Oregon town, Merri didn't have many places to go.

The adrenaline wore off. The vicious burn unbearable.

Miss Silver thought she heard a knock at the door. There it was again; soft almost muffled.

"Why, hi Merri... Merri what's wrong?"

"I'm hurt."

Miss Silver had been Merri's 6th-grade teacher and this pupil, now a grown woman, stood barely upright at her front door. In one hand a battered suitcase, the other hand wrapped in a dirty handkerchief. Merri stark white, trembling, going into shock.

"I don't know where to go."

Miss Silver got Merri in the car and, on the way to the hospital, heard what happened. On her own Miss Silver, at the admission desk, said Merri had a kitchen accident. Merri caught the lie and accepted it.

Merri was in the ER for a good while. She emerged, highly medicated, with a thickly bandaged hand. Miss Silver got her back in the car, back to her house and into the guest bed.

The doctor said there would be a scar, which proved true. Twenty-five years later, Merri Sue's first grandchild asked;

"Grandma, how did you hurt your hand?"

Merri said, "you be careful with hot pans in the kitchen, honey."

The grandchild followed that advice for the rest of her life.

In the morning, Miss Silver called the school to say she wouldn't be coming in for a few days. The vice-principal, a former pupil, said, "How on earth will I get a substitute on such short notice."

Miss Silver, drawing on her 30 years of experience teaching 6th grade and dealing with little piss-ants like this one replied;

"I don't know, but you'd better stop whining and get on it, right quick."

Merri Sue stayed with Miss Silver for a week. She improved, but the hand still hurt. Meds took the edge off. Miraculously, the police did not show up at the door, although both women feared it would happen. Miss Silver found out through a deputy sheriff, another former student, that Merri's father had gone into the hospital in the next town and said drunk, he had a fall in the kitchen. His story; he hit his forehead on the stove and the back of his head when he hit the floor. He was released after four days with a bill that would never be paid.

After much discussion, Miss Silver and Merri came up with a plan for Merri's future. Miss Silver called the high school counselor who had told her about a new federal program called the Job Corps on the coast in Astoria. After some intense lobbying by the counselor and high school principal, both former students of Miss Silver, Merri was accepted at the Job Corps and would begin in a month. Miss Silver found Merri a job in Portland until then with another former student, who needed help with her unruly 8-year-old twins.

Miss Silver paid for Merri's hospital bill. But Merri would need clothes, a better jacket, shoes, and money for her time at the Job Corps. All beyond Miss Silver's budget. The next Sunday at the church she had attended for 50 years, Miss Silver addressed the congregation with the problem and the need. Naming no names (but it was a small town, everybody knew) she asked a special offering to be made. The offering tray was sent around and returned to Miss Silver, who after a quick count, said the tray would be sent around again and she wanted people to give like they meant it this time. If she had to send it around the third time, there would be hell to pay. She said it loud and clear, in a teacher's voice;

"Literally, hell to pay."

4

THE BUS RIDE FROM EASTERN OREGON to Portland, dreary and long at first, turned beautiful. Merri knew the dry, burnt-out look of the high desert in Eastern Oregon, but Portland was different. Everything green. Pristine.

People talked about how much it rained in Portland. But that wasn't the case this summer. The whole season was golden. Cool in the early mornings, sometimes a little cloudy, then in the afternoon, glorious sunshine. The sky, the trees, Mt. Hood in the distance. All of it beautiful.

Merri liked the Clintons, the family she worked for, and loved the twins. They were a bit of trouble at first, but Merri won them over. The boys minded Merri Sue but didn't mind their parents. On Saturday, Merri's day off, and the parents in charge, the twins turned into a couple of wild Indians until Merri came back.

What Merri enjoyed most about her new living conditions was being someplace normal & calm. The twin's antics wore down their parents, but not Merri. She was a natural with kids. She had her own room, but it wasn't where she spent a lot of time.

Merri ate with the family, and after the first week, did most of the cooking. In the morning, Merri got the kids up, dressed them, made breakfast and their lunches, and walked them to school. The parents, who both worked, were a bit frantic when Merri first arrived. With her help, they calmed down and now enjoyed their time with the twins and Merri.

Merri spent the days grocery shopping, cleaning, cooking, and a little exploration of Portland. She loved downtown; the hustle and bustle, the tall buildings, beautiful store windows filled with wonderful clothes.

In the afternoon, she picked the boys up at school and walked them home. One hour of play time, then homework. When their parents got home; dinner, a bit of TV, bath and off to bed.

Each day was the same as the last, exactly what Merri needed. The parents begged Merri to stay. Tempting. But she had a plan, to go to the Job Corps and make something of her life. She was going there to find her way.

But she did mention it to Miss Silver on their weekly phone call. Miss Silver's reply was brisk;

"We made a plan and you will be sticking to that plan. You will be going to the Job Corps if I must carry you there."

Merri did not bring it up again.

5

MERRI TOOK THE 6 AM GREYHOUND BUS from downtown Portland to Astoria on Highway 26, the Sunset Highway. She got to the bus depot at 5:30 am. At that time of the morning, downtown Portland had lost all its glamour. The bus stopped in Hillsboro and then again at a roadside café called Staley's. From there over the Coast Range mountains.

As the bus started up the long grade, the sun came out and remained out for the rest of the trip. The evergreen trees, dripping wet from a recent shower, were a deep, brilliant green. The highway went over three or four streams, the water dazzling in the sunlight.

Well into the mountains there was a longer stop at a restaurant, bar, and motel called the Elderberry Inn. The roadside attraction there was a huge 16-foot-wide frying pan on top of the restaurant. Merri glanced down at the scar on her hand. The stop long enough for a cup of coffee. Not coffee like Merri would make. More like it was made by someone who didn't know what good coffee tasted like.

Then back on the bus and the next stop Seaside. Merri thought Seaside was exactly what Coney Island would look like. A beach town with one long main drag that went from the highway to a grand turnaround overlooking the broad beach. Small motels, curio shops, bumper cars, mini-golf, and salt water taffy. Still bustling with the end-of-summer crowds.

Then a short stop in Warrenton and finally Astoria. Coming across the 'new' Young's Bay Bridge, Merri could see that Astoria was a large peninsula, with Youngs Bay on one side and the Columbia River on the other. Astoria was all hills. Steep hills, with some grand Victorian houses and others that were Victorian but a bit worse for wear. These were mixed with smaller homes, post-World War II, all of them, elegant and plain, clinging to the hillside and steep streets.

Astoria could look a little damp & depressing on a wet day in January, but on a gloriously sunny day in August, it was a jewel.

On top of the tallest hill was the Astor Column, a 185-foot monument to the opening of the West. Merri would learn later that a person, if they were brave and had no fear of heights, could climb the inside, circular staircase to the top of the Column. Stepping outside onto a narrow landing, one could see West to the ocean; north to the Willapa Hills across the Columbia River in Washington state; East to a never-ending forest of green trees and South to Saddle Mountain. A view of 40 to 50 miles in every direction.

The Greyhound bus went under the brand-new Astoria-Megler Bridge, incredibly tall, spanning the Columbia, connecting Oregon & Washington. The bridge was four miles long, with a graceful turn away from the water and then a curve back to the River and a huge main span under which the biggest and tallest ships in the world could pass. The roadway on the highest part of the bridge was 200 feet above the water. Above that were two towering arches that rose more than 100 additional feet.

The bridge was something to see and Merri was amazed by it. To her, it looked like a giant piece of sculpture. Three and a half years in the building, it opened in 1966. Astoria was still in awe of the Bridge.

After the Bridge, the highway turned into the main street of Astoria. The bus went through the downtown core and then to the depot.

31

The bus depot was tacked on the side of the John Jacob Astor Hotel. The Hotel, at nine stories, was the tallest building in Astoria. Admittedly the Hotel was more than a little worn down. The once fabulous lobby, now leaning toward shabby, featured a bar/restaurant, the Fur Trader, a coffee shop and, above it, 126 rooms and suites.

Getting her one suitcase, Merri walked outside to the corner of 14th & Commercial Streets. She had 20 minutes to wait for her ride to the Job Corps.

Merri looked north on 14th one block and saw the Columbia River. An enormous freighter passed very close to shore almost like a part of downtown.

The Kobayashi Maru, an enormous freighter at 562 feet long, towered tall at 125 feet off the water. Moving silently, it headed east up the Columbia to Portland. As the ship passed the buildings of downtown Astoria, the superstructure loomed over the mostly two-story roofs. The freighter had left Kashima, Japan 21 days and 4,400 miles ago and passed over the Columbia River bar, one of the most dangerous in the world.

185 wrecks over the years in and around the Columbia River bar proved the point.

The ship would now navigate the 126-miles-long Columbia River channel to Portland, where it would load a cargo of wheat, grown in the Palouse area of eastern Washington State.

Standing at the corner of 14th & Commercial, Merri glanced upward at the peeling, fading pink façade of the John Jacob Astor. The sunshine gave it a weird, almost comical tint.

Merri Sue at that moment decided she liked Astoria.

The small bus marked *US Government, Job Corps*, picked Merri up at the Hotel and took her east for four miles to Tongue Point. The Point, a peninsula sticking out from shore into the Columbia River, was much smaller than the peninsula Astoria perched on. Tongue Point, 2 ½ miles long, ¾ of a mile wide nearest the shore, tapered to a heavily forested and undeveloped sharp point.

Merri was dropped off at the Job Corps Administration building where the head of Admissions waited to give her and four other incoming students their Introductory Tour. The first stop, the student living quarters, pleasantly surprised Merri. The large, but spartan, room had two beds on one side with built-in drawers on the other wall and a compact bathroom.

Next, the dining area and kitchen where Merri would spend the next three weeks on KP duty. The Culinary

Arts program students help staff the kitchen and ran The Bistro, the on-site restaurant.

From there on to the Learning Center.

Merri had a high school diploma, but the Job Corps would test her on English, mathematics, and general science knowledge, just to be sure no further studies were required. Merri would have the option (and encouragement) to attend the Clatsop College in Astoria to acquire an Associated Arts degree.

The last part of the tour had a visit to each of the different career path taught at the Tongue Point Job Corps; Culinary Arts, a Commercial Painting, Landscaping, Dental Assistance, Bookkeeping, Welding, and Electrical.

At each discipline, the Admissions Director asked a student to tell the group what the discipline and program were like. In the Commercial Painting, Kristen pointed to Penny Nichols.

At 4' 11", 158 pounds, Penny was always on a diet. With red hair and a very pale complexion, Penny blushed crimson whenever she drew attention. Growing up, she was always the last one chosen for grade school playground teams. In high school, Penny had few friends, never went to a prom, nor on a date. She hated the term 'wallflower.' It was how she thought of herself. All of that changed at the Job Corps.

Dressed in white painter's pants, shirt, and a painter's hat (during classes, all students dressed appropriately for their trade) Penny stood up, acknowledged Kristen, and shook hands with all the new students. She took a couple of steps back. In a clear voice, Penny said,

"My name is Penny Nichols. I am enrolled in the Commercial Painting program here at the Tongue Point Job Corps. I have been here for eleven months and in another seven months, I will graduate with a GED certificate, a trade, and a job with the Painters Union. If you can tough out three weeks of 'boot camp' here, you can achieve this too."

Penny had found her way.

Penny was Merri's first friend at Job Corps.

PART TWO
The People's Army

6

Just before Christmas in 1922

DISASTER STRUCK ASTORIA. The downtown district was built over the water's edge atop wooden pilings that would be kindling for a fire that razed the town. Headline:

ASTORIA, ORE. IS FIRE RUIN.
BUSINESS DISTRICT OF COAST CITY WIPED OUT.
FULL SWAY TO FLAMES FOR TEN HOURS, CAUSING A LOSS ESTIMATED AT FIFTEEN MILLION DOLLARS -- RELIEF MEASURES BEGUN.

By the Associated Press. Astoria, Ore., Dec. 8, -- The business district of Astoria, the *oldest city in Oregon, is in ruins, hundreds of persons are homeless and property loss estimated around $15,000,000 was caused by a fire here today. For ten hours the flames held sway, eating an ever-widening path thru the city until shortly after noon....*

No word of discouragement was heard on the streets of Astoria today. A forward looking spirit prevailed. In his battered office in the scorched and battered city hall, its ceilings dripping water and its windows partly shattered and still giving way periodically to thundering detonations from ruins across the street, Mayor JAMES BREMNER has this to say:

"We've got no town left, but we've still got the best harbor on the Pacific coast. We will start rebuilding at once on the old site. These things have happened before, to us once, to San Francisco, to Chicago and many other cities. Yet folks have gone ahead and built bigger and better cities on the ruins. We hope to do just that."

Mayor James Bremner's prognosis for the city's future came to pass; Astoria's business district was rebuilt, better than ever, this time atop a cement framework in place of the wooden pilings. The new structure created tunnels and basements beneath the streets and sidewalks. Thirty-eight years after the fire, this would become the playground and an inspiration for the creation of the People's Army.

7

PETE ARO, AN AVERAGE KID, got middling grades, lots of C's, every now & again a B, but never a D. He had a few friends, not a lot but enough. Since kindergarten, Bill Nikula was his best friend. Around the 4th grade, Joe Lagerstrom became a junior member of the Pete and Bill group.

In junior high, Tom Thompson became a somewhat regular member of the group.

In high school and before, Pete got in the appropriate amount of trouble, in school & out, for a typical Astoria kid. Several Parent/Teacher conferences, a more severe meeting with the high school Principal once. But nothing serious, no expulsions, no run-ins with the police. Pete went through his kid years and teens, not necessarily smoothly, but without leaving too much of a wake. His parents were thankful.

In fact, Pete wasn't all that exemplary of a kid, he just didn't get caught. Tom got caught a lot. Pete's parents felt sorry for Tom's parents.

With Pete's C grades and his parent's income, a state college, most likely the University of Oregon in Eugene was the best idea.

That's when everything changed.

On a beautiful fall day in September, Pete's parents packed the Ford station wagon and drove their son to Eugene. A big day for everybody. Pete's room at the dormitory was, of course, on the 3rd floor, with no elevator access.

Pete's roommate seemed like a nice young man. His parent's thought Pete equally nice, both sets of parents happy and proud. His mother Audrey, crying, hugged her son goodbye. Peter Jr and Sr shook hands.

The fall turned to winter and Pete, dazed & confused and wildly out of place, got into the rhythm of college life. Some of the courses were of interest and others he hated. He liked Eugene, enjoying his new freedom and at the same timed missed the familiarity of Astoria and his parents.

The family kept in touch. The weekly phone call; a good way to catch up and a good chance for Pete to ask for more money. Even at a state school, the tuition and Pete's living expenses cut into the Aro's budget.

But his parents were generous to their only child with both time and money. They drove down for almost all the U of O football games, Parents Day and Pete took the bus to Astoria for Thanksgiving and Christmas breaks and on some weekends when he ran out of clean clothes.

The first time Pete showed up with an enormous duffle bag of dirty clothes, Audrey spent all that Saturday; washing, drying, and folding. The next time it happened, she threw the dirty clothes and her son in the station wagon, gave him a pile of quarters, and dropped him at the laundromat.

The Summer of Love lasted for more than a summer: it went on for a couple of years. San Francisco was the epicenter, but Eugene, Oregon was well-known by the flower children of Aquarius. Ken Kesey, the novelist, had put Eugene on the map. As Kesey and his gang of merry pranksters moved on to San Francisco, Tom Wolfe, in his reporting, added to the Kesey legend and to the mystic of his hometown in southern Oregon.

This 'Hippie Movement' was about living & loving freely, if that tumultuous time and people could be described as a movement. The abandonment of ambition, greed & career. The search for inner knowledge & fulfillment. To be sure, casual sex, good dope, and great music made a big part of the mix.

Free Love, 'Good Lovin', Sports Sex; whatever you called it, was abundant. And to his surprise, Pete got his share.

Eugene had it all. Lots of kids with flowers in their hair, sandals on their feet, VW micro-buses, and everybody had a dog. Patchouli, marijuana, and the Grateful Dead filled the air. A comfortable, soothing, safe vibe, like a glorious spring morning, floated over it all.

And Pete floated right along with it.

When the fall/spring University year ended in June and Pete got his first-year grades, he called his parents with the good news. Pete told his parents he had gotten his usual grades of C's. He hadn't but felt what his parents didn't know, wouldn't hurt them.

Pete also announced that he would stay in Eugene for the summer semester, graduate sooner, and the savings would be helpful to his parents. In addition, the Aro's had become used to having the house to themselves and looked forward to not having a teenage boy sprawled across their couch all day, eating enormous amounts of food.

Pete wasn't altogether truthful with summer semester either. Yes, he would take courses but what really prompted the lie was something else. His well-mannered roommate, Jackson, had a side job of selling high-grade marijuana which he imported from Northern California to Eugene in the trunk of his VW bug. Pete had made the trip with Jackson a couple times and had made deliveries and other odd jobs.

Pete brought up an idea to Jackson late one night.

"Jack, what you need is a partner. With two people dealing, we can really crank this thing up."

"Well first off, Pete, I don't think of myself as a drug dealer. I'm more of a distributor."

"Good point. But you still need help. With one of us bringing the pot up and the other one 'distributing' it, we could triple the take." Pete wanted this deal.

"I agree, but I need to know what you can invest in your idea. If we triple the amount of pot coming in, we're gonna need more cash. They won't front the pot for us. What'd you got?"

"I got $700 in cash, for summer enrollment, class fees & books," Peter replied.

"Welcome aboard, partner!"

And that's how it started. By the end of the summer semester, Jackson or Peter made a weekly trip to Humboldt County, in northern California. By October, Pete had bought a used but nicely-maintained station wagon. He told his parents he paid $350 for it, out of money he made at the pizza parlor. Pete paid $1,500 for it out of his drug earnings. The pizza job was long gone.

At the beginning of 1969, Pete & Jackson moved out of the dorm and into a rental house near the U of O campus. At first, they mowed the lawn, kept to themselves, didn't have many people over and went through the motions of two college students working hard at their studies.

In fact, they were hardly studying at all and rolling in cash. By this time Eugene (and the rest of the country) was awash in drugs, mostly pot, but newer and harder drugs started to appear. Peter & Jackson had only one product; the best marijuana in Eugene, also the most expensive. Their clientele was a curated group; students with wealthy parents, local musicians, restaurant & bar workers, bored housewives, and trusted friends. They also had two resellers, one in Grants Pass & one in Roseburg. These two would drive to Eugene monthly to pick up three to five pounds to sell. Pete and Jackson gave the resellers a price break for the volume but never divulged the source of the weed.

The only drawback to having the most expensive dope in town was that it kept their potential customer base limited. Jackson was fine with that. He wanted to keep everything neat and contained. If things got too big, the police would hear about it, the last thing Jackson wanted. Keep the side hustle on the down low; high class, high profit and simple.

Pete disagreed. Most of his friends couldn't afford the weed he peddled. Keeping the quality & price high meant a slim audience. Keep the high price weed & then add a lower priced strain and you could sell everybody. That was Pete's business plan and he did just that. Without telling Jackson.

The source for the cheaper pot was a guy in Blue River, east of Eugene on the McKenzie River. Pete met him at a Robert Cray Band concert at the Overland Theatre in Eugene. Pete drove to Blue River weekly for product and on one of these trips, he met another guy in Thurston who supplied hash & hash oil. From there he met another guy who sold the new drug LSD.

Pete kept the new products secretly in his car. The Dodge station wagon became a rolling pharmacy. He made other changes.

Pete started using his own products.

A lot of product.

Started selling out of the rental house.

Jackson's idea was to deliver the dope to the client, never have them come to the rental. Pete tired of the hassle of setting appointments to drop off dope.

"Just come on over, dude."

People showed up at all hours of the day and night wanting to score. Jackson grew angry with the constant traffic flow. When he found out about the cheaper weed, the hash, and the LSD, he was furious and done with Pete.

The lease for the rental house was in Jackson's name. He moved all the pot out of the basement, into his VW and got the shoe boxes of money out of his closet. Then he paid off the rest of the lease in cash, threw all of Pete's belongings into a dumpster behind the A&W drive-in and checked into the Eugene Hilton.

Jackson called his parents in San Francisco that night to tell them he had discovered his roommate was a drug-dealing criminal he had barely escaped from. He told them he would drive home the next day. On the drive south on I-5 he sold half of the pot to the reseller in Roseburg and half to the one in Grants Pass. He told both that Pete was a Eugene PD informant.

Jackson transferred his meager academic credits to the University of San Francisco and after four years there and another two years at Berkley got his law degree. He invested the Eugene drug money in a California real estate fund. With that sizeable sum, he started his law practice in Mountain View, south of San Francisco.

Both his practice and investments centered on the growing 'dot.com' industry. Jackson saved the mid-sized fortune he made during those boom years, by bailing out of dot.com just before the bust. Jackson retired at 42 and lives today in Hillsborough where he grows orchids and invests in new technologies.

Things turned out differently for Pete. He got back to the Eugene rental house after a day trip to Blue River, his station wagon loaded with pot. The house dark, his key wouldn't unlock the door. No sign of Jackson. Finally, he broke his bedroom window, badly cutting his hand. Blood dripping, Pete went from room to room.

All his things gone.

The shoebox 'banks' gone.

All the high price dope in the basement, gone.

Pete checked into the Eugene Commercial Motel on a weekly rate. The next day he came back to the house. The landlord nailed plywood over the broken window and a police car sat in the driveway. Pete thought about reporting the theft of his things and money to the cop. Then thought better of it.

In the next few weeks the money Pete had kept in his own 'bank,' the glove box in the Dodge, started to run out. He had to check out of the motel. Started serially couch crashing at various friends. Living arrangements were loose. There always seemed to be a couch, a living room rug and even sometimes a bed and sometimes someone to share it with.

For Pete, college life began to be a distant memory. He kept up the pretense for his parents. His weekly phone calls to brag about his nonexistent grades (he had stopped going to classes months ago) continued. He asked that his parent's checks go to a PO box. Pete told his parents he worried about mail being stolen from the box at the rental house. He didn't want to tell his parents he wasn't living with Jackson anymore.

Mr. Aro and Audrey had been planning to come to Parent's Day, but Audrey's bunion surgery conflicted with the date. When they called Pete with the news, he sounded relieved. It hurt Audrey's feelings. She suggested he come home that weekend instead. Pete couldn't, the bus trip too long. Pete had sold the station wagon to front a load of weed from a new source. The deal never worked out and Pete lost the money.

The bunion surgery got postponed; the doctor's wife gave birth to a four-pound baby girl, four weeks premature. Pete Sr. and Audrey thought it would be fun to surprise Peter on Parent's Day. The drive down to Eugene, a long one, both parents looking forward to a nice weekend with their son and his charming roommate.

The Aros stopped first at the rental house. No Peter, no Jackson. The young couple living there knew nothing about previous tenants. Their only information was that the rental had been a 'drug house.' The next stop the Parent's Day Welcome Center; no luck there either. They placed a hurried call to the Registrar's office and after a brief meeting, Pete Sr. and Audrey learned their son had stopped going to classes 8 weeks ago. His roommate, Jackson, dropped out of the university three months ago.

The last stop was the Eugene Police station downtown. A kind, but slightly bored police Sergeant took their information. The Aros stayed in Eugene overnight, waiting for the mandatory 24 hours until a Missing Person report could go out.

8

WHEN PETE'S FRIENDS, MONEY AND LUCK ran out in Eugene, he followed friends to the Sunrise commune deep in the woods east of town. Pete wasn't looking for 'Peace, Love & Understanding.' He needed somewhere to hang out, stay high, and find girls. He wanted to "just relax, man, it's been a tough couple of months." All of this needed to be free. Pete had no money left.

If he had to put up with some hippie 'mumbo-jumbo' to meet his modest goals, that was fine. In fact, he believed in a lot of that 'jumbo.' Pete's hippie leanings had a political bent. His favorite course at U of O, Political Science. He was thinking of making Poli Si his major before drug distribution got in the way.

Pete's political stance was consistent with the times and his age group.

"The Man has screwed me royally. Me and a bunch of other people. Something must be done. And it will. You watch, man; it'll happen."

What had to be done was never known.

The Sunshine commune had been founded years ago. No one seemed to know when. It was somebody's great-grandparents land. The site sat next to Gale Creek a tributary of the McKenzie River, outside of the village of Vida. The creek provided drinking water, clothes washing, fishing, and skinny dipping. The commune-maintained pit toilets at an appropriate distance from the two dozen tents and lean-to shacks that provided housing for the group. Under an ancient oak sat a kitchen station with a giant canopy to protect it from the weather. There had been a cabin, but it burned down during a New Year's Eve celebration.

Commune members and visitors followed a loose list of duties and responsibilities. Some members kept these guidelines religiously, and others, not at all.

Things at Sunshine changed when the great-grandparents died. Then, various aunts, uncles, and lawyers got involved. It turns out 65 acres of cleared grassland, graced with beautiful oak trees and a year-round creek was worth something. Worth quite a bit.

Neighbors near the commune were happy to hear something was happening; it might be shutting down.

Some neighborhood kids had wandered over there and didn't want to come back. The Sheriff had several calls about Sunrise and investigated rumors of drugs going in and out of the commune.

A survey party showed up first. Then lawyers and then the Sheriff.

But things at the commune had been going wrong for a while. Too many visitors, hangers-on, and some truly crazy people. Too many with different ideas that didn't mesh with the original members of Sunrise.

The commune divided into two separate groups; 'Peace & Love' and a harder edge, more radical set.

The radical group was drawn to the sex, drugs, and openness of the laid-back hippie lifestyle. But that's were the shared beliefs stopped. The radical group was into tearing things down or blowing them up. Either for political means, profit or for the sheer elation of 'Burning Down Amerikka.'

Pete gravitated to the more radical group. They had cars and drove into Eugene for drinks and concerts. Usually, Pete tagged along. A small group from somewhere in California showed up. It was three guys. Their leader, a scary looking dude with long dark hair, deep-set eyes, and a frightening Fu Manchu mustache. After trips into Eugene's nightlife with this group, Pete got the impression they weren't looking for drugs, but explosives. This group, not into Peace, Love or Understanding.

That group moved on after a few days and then another group, three guys and a girl from southern California passed through. Late one night they asked Pete if he knew of anyone looking for military-grade C-4. Hoping to make it with the girl (not a chance,) Pete was surprised by the question. He never knew if the two California groups got together.

When the Sheriff came back to Sunrise, he came with deputies and a writ saying that everyone had to be out in 48 hours. After that, anyone left would be arrested and their belongings confiscated. Commune members with outstanding warrants left first.

Within the 48 hours, everyone joined them. Leaving a hellacious mess.

Some traveled to a commune east of Ashland, near Lake of the Woods. Others headed for Big Sur. Some moved to a Clatsop County camp in the woods near Astoria, Oregon. And others just went into the wind.

Pete thought of the Clatsop camp near Astoria, his hometown. But he tired of the commune life. He hitch-hiked to Astoria to make amends with his parents.

It didn't go the way he expected.

"Son, your Mother and I think you have made your own bed and now you need to lay in it. We don't have a place for you now. Get a job, get cleaned up, we can talk then."

With absolutely no place to go, Pete went back to what he knew; his childhood friends, Bill & Joe. And the three moved in together, always one step ahead of the rent, through a series of rooms to rent and small apartments until they found a rent-free squat in east Astoria.

9

BILL AND PETE HITCHHIKED BACK to Astoria from the Perrina's mink ranch. Fired, again. Bill and Pete always worked as a team. Not a great team, not even good or mediocre team; a hapless, bumbling collaboration that had been going on since grade school.

They lived their day-to-day lives as if they were already 3 drinks in and eagerly awaiting their 4th. And usually, they were either stoned, drunk or both. Friends and co-conspirators since second grade, Bill and Pete had been fired exactly as many times as they had been hired.

"All I wanted was a little shut-eye."

"Where did he find you?"

"Under the cages in barn five. Said he could smell the pot."

"What pot?"

"The pot in the band-aid box, under the sink at the house."

"Hell, that's my pot, my emergency stash."

"I was gonna share it with you but couldn't find you. I only smoked a little."

"Well give me back the rest."

"I hid it in the cage above my head."

"Dammit, the mink ate it. So, nothing to smoke when we get back. Thanks."

"I got my emergency stash in the cigar box behind the stove. I'll share it with ya."

"Big of you."

They weren't all that upset about losing the job. They had worked at Mr. Perrina's mink farm for five weeks, a record. Bill and Pete had been dishwashers, painters, movers, plumber helpers, construction hands, gardeners, lawn mowers, refuse haulers, delivery guys, grocery stockers, newspaper boys, tree planters.

Mr. Perrina had been good to them. A nice Finnish guy who ran a tight farm. He paid a good wage for a good day's work. The wages worked for Bill & Pete; the actual work, not so much.

Mink are smallish, mean little bastards, with luxurious coats. They will bite a person viciously if given any chance. Driven literally mad when caged, they move constantly in their wire enclosures. Snarling and hissing, they try to bite each other and anything else that comes close.

Mink are caged separately and fed a foul mixture of fish parts, chicken parts, and grain. Bill and Pete would drive Perrina's flatbed truck into Astoria to the canneries (They told Perrina they had driver's licenses. They didn't, both suspended) to get the fish guts, fish scales, bones and who knows what other grisly fish parts from the fish canneries. The cannery stuffed and froze this unholy mess in burlap sacks which Bill and Pete threw on the truck and tied them down.

Next stop, the chicken processing plant for that disgusting frozen concoction. Almost the same, but chicken parts instead of fish, frozen burlap bags thrown on to the truck. Then back to the mink farm.

Since they didn't tie the load down well, the load was always lighter getting off the truck than on. Fish and chicken byproducts were mixed with grain and water in an ancient cement mixer and poured into giant buckets which went onto wheeled carts. Bicycle tires made pushing the carts a bit easier going uphill and downright uncontrollable going downhill. Many near misses, collisions, and disgusting crack-ups with the side of barns; fish guts and chicken parts, like a soup made by Satan, covering everything.

A day on a Mink farm was physically hard, smelly, at times disgusting. In winter extremely cold, and in the summer sweltering. A tough job for anybody. For Bill and Pete; hungover, grumpy, sleep deprived, it was a stumbling step into Hell and back.

Getting a ride back to Astoria took a bit longer than Bill and Pete had hoped. It turns out two, dirty, smelly guys, after a half day of work on a mink ranch, aren't the most desired set of hitchhikers.

After walking backward, thumbs out, for a mile, they got a ride from a delivery van. After promising to take them all the way to Upper Town (east Astoria), instead, the driver demanded they get out at Miles Crossing, two miles south of town. The dirt and dishevelment didn't bother the driver, but the guy's appalling smell gagged him.

They had a mile and a half walk to the old Young's Bay Bridge. The bridge, built in the 1920s was barely wide enough for a couple Model T's, much less modern cars and trucks and a constant stream of log trucks. Without a sidewalk, Bill & Pete crept sideways across the bridge, running when a break in traffic occurred.

From there on, a long, desultory march to their destination on 39th Street and the need for a functioning car mentioned almost every step of the way.

Bill & Pete squatted in the basement of a once grand Victorian house.

Built in 1902 for the Gilbert family, the owner of Astoria's leading department store. The Gilberts already had a beautiful home, but Mrs. Gilbert didn't feel it truly reflected the style and wealth of one of Astoria's leading families. The new home stood three stories high (not counting the basement) and was a monument to turn of the century elegance. It had a beautiful porch, grand 10-foot high front door and a color scheme that used eight different colors.

The inside was every bit as grand as the outside, the woodwork intricate and beautiful. Banisters, doorways, windows, all done in the best mahogany and teak. A team of six artisans from Belgium created the plaster ceilings and cornices. The architect was from San Francisco and the general contractor, from Seattle, brought his own team of 12 with him. They worked on the house for 18 months.

The only work done by locals was the most menial and labor-intensive kind.

The Gilbert department store, founded in 1875, sold everything from rope to millenary, hardware to housewares, Levis to linens. It burned down in the fire of 1922. The owners rebuilt the store, but the business never regained its past success. The Depression killed it. It lingered on through the early 1930s, but really died in 1929.

From there, Mrs. Gilbert's beautiful home fell on hard times. A couple of buyers tried to bring it back to life, but in each case, it was too expensive. It became a rental, some sort of a boarding house and then a deserted house and a public nuisance. Still standing but ruined.

Bill & Pete didn't know who lived upstairs and thought it better not to ask. It was a true 60's sort of living arrangement. Bill & Pete needed a roof and not much more and the basement filled that need. The fewer questions asked, the better.

After the day they had been through, a shower would have been ideal. Unfortunately, no shower, no tub. Only a cast iron sink, with cold water, not hot. The toilet was at the other end of the basement, in the open. Like a silent sentinel.

The basement unfinished, to say the least, had no interior walls, just one small window, a door, and a massive amount of junk. Bill took one corner of the cramped space and Pete had another. Joe the 3rd roommate was at work. Unlike his pals, Joe had and could keep a job. His space was beside the nonworking oil furnace.

The basement resembled a forest floor; layers and layers of duff, some of it new, some ancient. The top layer mostly the flotsam & jetsam of Bill, Pete, and Joe's daily lives. It was a thin but growing, crispy layer of fast food wrappers, beer bottles, the odd whiskey fifth, clothes, shoes, garbage never taken out, Playboy magazines, cigarette butts and who really knew what else. During the rainy season—in Astoria, November through June—a small stream meandered through parts of the basement.

Women who came over never stayed long.

Scattered throughout, over & under this mess was a full set of golf clubs; a drum set, buried deep but easily stumbled over on a late-night trip to the toilet; a TV, radio, phonograph console that didn't work, but served as a stand for a small black & white TV; a Hammond B4 organ, a croquet set; basketball hoop; a mostly complete set of Colliers encyclopedias; a small refrigerator from the Truman administration era, a much older stove; several broken chairs, lamps and a couch that had a tie-dyed cover. The couch which everyone said was still there hadn't been seen in months.

64

The actual floor, never seen.

After a brisk spits bath, armpits and face, Bill and Pete set about the main part of every evening – smoking pot. Pete's emergency stash presumed behind the stove was under the refrigerator. That took an hour to find. The rolling papers were never found. The bong took another 45 minutes to unearth. At last, Bill & Pete—stoned and at peace and sitting on an unbelievably dirty mattress—watched TV.

The black and white TV Pete found at a yard sale but never paid for. Just walked away with it. Astoria was too far away from any TV station or broadcast tower for almost any antenna to work. Portland being the closest at 100 miles, Seattle much further. But Astoria became the first American city with cable TV. A powerful antenna on top of the John Jacob Astor Hotel pulled in the Portland stations. At first, the images went only to the Fur Trader bar in the lobby. Later, out to nearby businesses, homes, and then wires were strung throughout the city and the cable TV business was born.

Astoria was not only the first American city with cable TV; it was the first American city with a group of citizens who thought cable should be free. In some neighborhoods, if one house had and paid for cable, the rest of the street had it for free. The small TV Bill and Pete watched was torturously wired through a couple of backyards to a cable wire on the next block.

When they grew tired of the TV, Pete turned to his favorite topic of conversation after women, booze, drugs and how to acquire more of each; politics. A rant that went on forever.

10

"THE NIGHTLIFE, IT AIN'T NO GOOD LIFE," Bill sang in a mumbled manner, "But it's my—"

Peter looked back at him as they walked down Exchange Street in downtown Astoria. The sun had set, the river breeze crisp, and the trio of guys was half-lit and preparing to go all the way.

"What is that you're singing?"

"Ah, it's coming out by Willie Nelson later this year." Bill relished knowing something that Peter did not. "I told you my brother was a DJ, right?"

At least a dozen times, the lanky Peter thought.

"Well, when Willie gets to the San Francisco area, they hang out. He gave my brother an advance promo copy."

Peter stared at Bill as he scratched his anemic red beard. He decided to let the topic die, and the guys turned right 15th Street.

There, at the northwest corner of Duane and 15th, lay an open pit in the ground a half block square. After the town's fire of 1922, the town was rebuilt, higher than water level and atop cement pillars and beams. Streets and buildings rested on this structure. But not this half block. It was never covered. The other half of the block was the bus terminal which abutted the John Jacob Astor Hotel, both street level.

The pit sloped down from the southern end bordering Duane Street to the sandy beach soil at Commercial Street at the northern end. Dense, thorny blackberry bushes covered the pit.

The guys headed down a broken path overgrown with blackberry bushes with confidence and experience despite the threatening thorns. At the northwest corner of the pit, a gate was the only opening in a chain-link wall that surrounded the lot.

Ivy growth clung to the fence shielding the underground of Astoria from unknowing eyes. But behind the fence, a damp, cold world existed. The smell of the river mixed with the scent of unused, deserted spaces. Silent, hidden away. Sewer pipes laid out over the sandy floor. Dripping water lines attached to the ceiling made an eerie sound as the drops landed in a puddle. An all-day darkness. The Columbia River two blocks away.

The guys headed directly to the padlocked gate. Its chain link sagged from the weight of underground intruders. Barbed wire, long ago snipped, hung defeated at either side. Peter and Bill hopped the gate with experienced ease entering the Astoria tunnels. Joe, a stocky young man with a few excess pounds, executed the climb over with less grace than his buddies.

As they walked to their usual hangout, the darkness grew, and some occasional vermin scattered about. Joe turned on his red plastic Ray-O-Vac flashlight. Bill began to sing again, then stopped to relight and take a drag on a doobie and passed it around. "It won't be released for a few months yet... but I like it."

"Uh huh," Peter, of little patience, muttered. He leaned against a cement pillar as he enjoyed a deep take on the joint. After a long, silent moment he spoke. "What are we doing, guys?"

Joe looked at Peter quizzically. "What we do every Friday night. Break into the tunnels and get screwed up."

"Exactly, Joe."

"I don't get you, man." Sometimes Peter confused Joe and now was one of those times.

"I mean," Peter went to the depths of his philosophical mind, "What are we doing?"

The other two looked at one another in silence for a second, not sure what their friend was talking about. When they could not stand the silence any longer, they burst out in laughter.

"Maybe," Joe said, "We need to cut you off. You're scaring me." He glanced Bill's way for backup.

"Joe's right. I'm lost."

"I mean, I mean, what are we doing?"

Again, the two looked at one another. Again, they broke into laughter.

Peter, his back still leaning against the rough cement pillar, slid down until he was sitting on the damp ground. "We need to do something."

"We are, Pete. We're getting screwed up."

"Yeah," Peter thought, "That's what I mean." More silence. "I mean, what are we going to do with our lives? Johnson is in power with the military-industrial complex backing him up. He's gonna send us all to Nam. Bob and Jack are hiding out in Canada. And here we are. But where are we? We need to cause change, right? We need to make the world a better place."

Bill thought about it from his clouded brain. "But, how?"

Peter pointed a finger his way as if Bill was on to something. After a moment, he had an idea. "We need to do more than sit-ins, guys. We need to really get the attention of the government. Make a statement. Not take 'no' for an answer." He thought a second and stared up at the cement ceiling that supported the downtown above it. They were sitting under the sidewalk of the John Jacob Astor Hotel and a light came on in his mind. He was always more creative when he was high.

"I might still have some connections down south. You know... guns... explosives."

"Jesus, Pete, what do you have in mind?" Bill wanted to know where in the hell this was going.

"We're going national, my friend, we're going national. Get the media's attention."

"Now that's what I'm talking about," Joe declared, "I'm in!" Joe admired Peter and easily followed him.

Bill looked at him a second. "I'm all for shaking things up, Pete, but explosives?"

"Don't worry. You're going to like it. I'll get hold of my friends. It'll go from there."

"Let's rock this world!"

Peter cocked his finger at Bill and the doobie he held and demanded he pass it to him. The stage was set. Their purpose decided. They would write history. Later, it would evolve into the People's Army... if they remembered it in the morning.

PART THREE
Evil Moves North

11

September 13, 1969

THE PLAN WAS SIMPLE; three into the bank, two in the get-away car and one in the backup car. Two AK-15s and a shotgun into the bank. Another AK and a sawed-off shotgun in the getaway. Andre had his two semi-auto pistols and a ridiculously big over/under shotgun as a backup. The pistols less than needed and the shotgun way more.

Andre was the mastermind and self-proclaimed leader. Older with jet-black hair and a Fu Manchu mustache; he found the jobs, did the planning, didn't do drugs. He knew the three guys going into the bank from Lodi High School in California that they all had attended, although none had graduated. They had been in and out of small-time crime, some jail time, and, except for Andre, a lot of drugs. This was to be their first big score.

The two in the getaway car were from a hippie/anarchist commune, Sunshine, in Eugene, Oregon. Andre had fallen into the collective the previous summer. Andre involved them in his plans based on their fast car, access to their parent's money, and a safe place to run to after the score. It worked that Eugene was out of state and the commune in the middle of nowhere. These two had big plans to use the money for large-scale terrorist attacks across the US. It would be the first actions of a plan to "set fire to the ruling class of Amerikka."

Andre didn't plan on them getting a cut, didn't plan on them getting back to Eugene at all, and couldn't have cared less about their terrorist pipe dreams. Once they robbed the bank and the money was safe, the two from Eugene would disappear along with their never-ending, mind-numbing political rants.

Andre had only one driving force; money. The best way to get money was to steal it. He'd tried working but hated it. Before that, he tried getting a high school diploma, only to fail. Joined the Army. Lasted three years of a four-year hitch.

In an Artillery Brigade at Fort Lewis, Andre received a Dishonorable Discharge for theft of Army ordinance. Andre's life vision now, if he had one, was to be a career criminal.

Andre had done his due diligence. The bank was old, in a downtown location, with an ornate interior with bad angles for surveillance cameras. The area had several restaurants, fast food joints and coffee shops. Heavy auto and pedestrian traffic made it better to blend into after the robbery.

At exactly noon, Andre drove Gabe, Leonard, and Smithy, the three going into the bank, down Main Avenue. The getaway car already in position.

Andre slowed down and stopped in front of the bank.

"OK now!"

The three put on black ski masks. Guns loaded, rounds racked, safeties off. Adrenaline running high.

The three out of the car and into the bank.

Smithy by the bank door, shotgun raised.

"This is a robbery. Get on the floor. Do not move. No one gets hurt."

Gabe in front of the teller's row. AK pointed head high at the first teller.

"Put all your money on the counter. Now."

Leonard, his AK pointed at the back of the bank manager's head.

"Open the vault. Now."

Andre had driven his car around the block and into a parking garage, up to the open top floor. His car running, Andre leaned over the railing to see the front of the bank on the opposite side of the street. The getaway car parked a block away, motor running.

Andre hoped the two in the getaway car would not screw this up. Benny and his girlfriend, Moonbeam or Asteroid or whatever her name, had been there for an hour in place, waiting. Motor running. They could be the weak link.

Andre was wrong, he was the weak link.

In all his planning, he neglected to notice that the Sacramento Chief of Police had lunch every weekday at the Lunch Counter across the street from the bank. The Chief didn't eat at the counter. He and his crew— the City Manager, the Sacramento State College football coach, and his parish Priest–all sat at the four-top table by the window.

Now Gabe had all the teller money stuffed into an over-sized duffle. All the tellers now on the floor with everyone else. Heads down. Gabe went to the vault area to check on the Manager and Leonard.

"Let's go!" Gabe shouted. "We need to get the hell out of here. What's taking you so long?"

"The bastard needed convincing."

The bank Manager slid down the doorway, bleeding from a bashing to his head, leaving a bloody trail down the side of the wall.

"Jesus."

"Here, take one of the bags," Leonard said. "I can't carry both."

Gabe set down the duffle full of teller money and picked up both vault money bags leaving the duffle behind. Gabe realized he had left it just as he ran out the bank's front door. By then it was too late.

The Assistant Manager didn't try to get up or even roll over. It was the sweat from the left side of his forehead streaming into his eye. He wanted to move his head off the floor enough to turn to the other side.

Smithy saw the movement. Jumpy, he turned his body and somehow the shotgun fired. The blast hit the Assistant Manager in the face. He died instantly. No one lives through that.

 At the sound of the shot, the security guard got to his feet. The blast from the other barrel of Smithy's shotgun tore into the guard's legs. He didn't die but wouldn't walk again either.

Gabe ran into the main area of the bank carrying the two bags of vault money and his AK, Leonard behind him.

"Stay down, dammit. Stay down."

But one of the tellers had lost it. She stood up, screaming. Gabe, dropping the money bags, let loose with his AK.

20 rounds traced high into the bank's walls and windows, above the teller's stations.

30 rounds waist high.

3 rounds caught the teller.

Smithy, screaming "Guys, let's go. Let's go."

Gabe, picking up the bags again, started to the front. Leonard stayed behind. He sensed something bad starting to happen. As Gabe and Smithy got to the door, they passed the security guard, bleeding badly but alive, and mad as hell. Adrenaline pumping, he reached for his gun. Not the service revolver the robbers had taken from his holster. That was the bank's. The guard reached for his own gun, known when he was on the Sacramento P.D. as a 'throw away' gun; what you used when you really needed it. He really needed it now.

Reaching for the Smith & Wesson 38 strapped to his ankle, the Guard thought he would up and die right there. The pain was unbelievable, indescribable. He took a long moment to gain his composure.

As Smithy and Gabe reached the front door of the bank, the getaway car slammed to a stop in front. Smithy down the first step outside. Gabe almost out the open door. The guard took his pistol in both hands, held a deep breath, and shut his right eye. He aimed and fired. The shot hit the back of Gabe's head, ending Gabe's life right then and there.

Across the street at the Lunch Counter, the Chief heard shotgun blasts and seconds later, a pistol shot. He jumped up, spilling everybody's lunch and coffee, and used his walkie to call in the alarm.

"Shots fired. Shots fired. Sacramento Savings and Loan, main branch. All units respond."

With that, the Chief was out the door, gun drawn, surveying the scene as he ran. A Dodge Charger slammed to a stop at the base of the bank's steps. A masked man, with a shotgun, two steps down the stairs. Another halfway out the bank's door.

As the first man on the stairs raised his shotgun at the Chief, the man behind him fell out of the doorway and down the stone steps. The Chief fought to process what he saw but it appeared the man was missing part of his head. The two black plastic bags the man carried burst open. Money flew around the stairs. A sudden burst of wind carried the money down the block like dry leaves in the wind.

It was all going wrong for Smithy. As the getaway car pulled up, a cop appeared out of nowhere. Gun drawn, raising it to shoot the hell out of Smithy. Smithy raised his shotgun, but he was too slow.

Something in the Chief's mind clicked. Everything slowed down. He could see the money blowing away, could see the man at the bottom of the bank stairs raise his shotgun. Firing over the hood of the Charger in front of him, the Chief hit the man twice, center mass. The man went down.

The two in the getaway got to the bank in time to hear the shot and see Gabe tumbling out of the bank. Saw Smithy raise his gun at the cop across the street. Smithy going down. The cop aiming at them now.

The girl in the passenger seat of the Charger, whose given name was Samantha Kettle, squirmed to aim the double-barreled shotgun out the driver's side window at the cop. She couldn't pull both triggers. Samantha chose the left one. The gun kicked back at her. Its blast hit Benny in the side of his face. The inside of the driver's side window turned red for an instant and crumbled away. Through the now open car window, Samantha saw the policeman and his gun pointed directly at her. Samantha's brain stopped. She froze, the shotgun still held level.

The Chief knew that both men on the stairs at the bank were down and out. His mind clicked that recognition. Next, his eyes and mind went to the Dodge Charger. Still running. Through the driver side window, he saw the male driver, beside him a female passenger and the double-barreled shotgun aimed directly at his head. As the Chief calculated all of this, he got calmer still. Almost peaceful. In the very back of his brain, the thought that he might die ticked away softly and slowly.

The driver's side window turned crimson, like a bucket of paint thrown at it, then the window shattered. The Chief saw the female, a child in his eyes, and her shotgun aimed at his head. Chief fired once. The bullet entered Samantha's left temple and exited through her right temple. Her shotgun clattered to the floor of the car, knocking the dead driver's foot off the brake. The car, still running, moved slowly forward, gently nudging the sides of a couple of parked cars and then coming to rest against a fire hydrant down the block.

The three shots the Chief fired were the first and last bullets he ever shot in his career.

Andre, on the top floor of the parking garage, leaning over the railing, saw a bad dream, a nightmare.

Everything going wrong. All the planning down the drain. All chances of the perfect score, gone. The two in the getaway car, most likely dead. Smithy and Gabe on the bank steps, surely dead as well.

Then, in an instant, Andre's thoughts shifted back to his own self-preservation. His survival. The cops didn't know anything about him. He hadn't gone into the bank during the robbery. When he did go into the bank for planning, he wore a disguise. All he had to do was keep calm and slip away.

Getting into the car, driving down the steep ramp, another thought came to Andre.

Where was Leonard and the rest of the money?

Andre had seen the two garbage bags full of money burst open on the Bank's steps. But he hadn't seen the duffle bag with the teller's cash. Left in the bank? Leonard hadn't come out yet. Was he alive? Dead?

And most importantly, did he have the money?

As Andre reached street level and turned onto the avenue, he thought of the alley behind the bank. If Leonard was alive, if he had the money, why couldn't he walk out the back door of the bank? Duffle bag under his arm, stuffed with cash, looking like another office worker on his way to the gym for his noon work out.

With this in his head, Andre slowed the car as he pulled past the mouth of the alley and saw Leonard, a block ahead, not running, but walking with a purpose.

Andre and Leonard drove through downtown Sacramento, got on Highway 99, and headed north.

Trading off driving, Andre and Leonard made it to Yreka in the late afternoon. In a cheap motel room straight out of the movie 'Psycho,' on one of the twin beds, they dumped out the money from the duffle bag; the 'teller money.' At first, the money made a nice, if somewhat small, pile. But as they counted it and recounted it, reality set in. The total - $27,500. Not much for a four-way split and now even with a two-way split, it was at best disappointing. Not the score of a lifetime; not the game changer they wanted. What it was… was measly. Only enough to get the 2 of them through a few months.

The arguing started immediately.

Andre - "All of the hard work and planning I did… all for 27K… what a—"

Leonard – "Maybe if we had another guy inside. Instead of a pussy, hanging over the railing across the street, like he was watching a stage play. Maybe if we had someone who wasn't afraid to get their hands a little dir—"

Andre – "What we did need was someone with an ounce of brains. I brought in Smithy & Gabe, who'd you bring in? A couple of space cadets that—"

Leonard – "I brought in kids that had money and a car and they were disposable."

Andre – "Well you sure disposed of them didn't you and the two bags of money they were supposed to drive away with. Nice work."

Leonard - "And Gabe & Smithy? How'd that work out? How'd your planning work out for them? How'd your precious planning work out for any of us?"

It went on like that until midnight. By then, they were both tired and sick of each other. But it was too late to do anything but jam the money back in the duffle and throw it in the corner.

September 14

In the morning, hunger drove them out of the motel, into the car and to the back booth at a diner in Hilt, California; almost to the Oregon border. At the end of the late breakfast, they agreed to head North and lie low. They needed to take some time and decide where the next score would be.

The original plan was to drive to the commune outside of Eugene that the two in the getaway car had come from. By now, neither Leonard nor Andre remembered their names. Andre thought they could hang there for a couple of weeks and come up with their next move, but trusting anyone at the commune, about anything, seemed less and less like a good idea. Too many loose lips, too many blissed-out beings.

Little did Leonard and Andre know; Sunshine was no more.

12

September 14

WHAT LEONARD AND ANDRE NEEDED was a place to 'chill.' From Hilt, they headed north on Interstate 5, Andre's black Pontiac GTO eating up the miles. Out of California and into Oregon over the Siskiyou Mountain range. Down the long grade into Ashland then on through Medford, Grants Pass, and Roseburg. It was cooler now, the scenery greener.

Leonard had started the day shaving off his beard, a disguise he grew for the bank job. Slender, almost diminutive at 5' 7" & 150 pounds, Leonard now thought the beard looked ridiculous. It had grown in thick and wooly, overpowering the rest of his face.

"So why the clean-shaven look?" Andre asked over the roar of the wind through his open driver's side window.

"Don't need it now. It was just a cover for the job."

"Who could see the beard under the ski mask? You should have worn a wig too."

There was no reply. These were the first words either had spoken in a hundred miles and if this was the way it would go, Leonard didn't even want to start. He was wondering how he got involved with this arrogant ass in the first place.

They finally stopped in Cottage Grove for a late lunch and a badly needed clearing of the air.

"OK, we both agree the commune isn't right for us," said Leonard.

Andre's terse reply, "Never was. OK, genius what is your idea now?"

"Glad you asked, Dip Shit. What we need to do is go for a deep chill. Get off I-5, head for the coast. Relax, spend a little of our money and after a couple of weeks, check out Eugene or Portland. Small jobs this time, no banks; too much trouble, too many guys needed. We go for jewelry stores, stuff like that, quick in and out."

It was the longest Andre had ever heard the little guy speak.

"Leonard, that's your grand plan? We turn into small-time stick-up guys. What the hell are you talking about? We'd have to do three or four jobs a month. All that risk and for what, pocket change? And the next time you call me Dip Shit, I'll kick your ass into next week. I'm not kidding."

"What I am talking about, Dip Shit, is a plan that doesn't leave at least 6 people dead and the town police, state police and FBI looking for who did it. That's the plan. If you don't like it, let's split up the money and go our own ways."

And so, it went for the next hour. They finally agreed they would head for the Oregon coast, relax and after a month or so, head to Portland doing small jobs while Andre planned the next big score.

Now that they had settled their differences (for the moment) they paid their check and walked on to the sidewalk and there it was, right across the street.

The Oregon Mutual Bank of Cottage Grove.

Waiting to be taken.

September 15

The planning to rob the bank in Cottage Grove started the next day. The difference in strategies was apparent. Andre left first on a search for a raincoat, hat, sunglasses, and notepad. Everything but the raincoat was easy to find. He found one at JC Penny, two sizes too small. It was all they had.

"Hey, Andre it's a perfect disguise for a guy casing a bank, you show up looking exactly like a guy casing a bank. Not a cloud in the sky and you show up in a raincoat. You look like a Dip Shit."

"You say that one more time, Leonard and you're dead." Andre walked out and slammed the motel door before Leonard could say it again.

After a leisurely breakfast, Leonard bought his disguise; a baseball cap and a pair of cheap sunglasses. The cap pulled low, Leonard entered the bank with a newspaper under his arm. He walked directly to the teller with the longest line.

As he waited, Leonard looked around and saw no sign of security cameras and no security guard. *Gotta love small towns*, Leonard thought. And there was Andre skulking around the edges of the bank lobby, making notes on a yellow pad. Leonard wondered

91

why he didn't just carry a sign 'Robber' and save everybody a lot of time.

Leonard saw the two teller stations, behind them the main vault, the assistant Manager's desk to one side of the vault and the Manager's office on the other side, behind a closed frosted glass door. He noticed that twice the teller in his line walked to a door next to the Manager's office. She opened the door, closed it, and came out with cash.

The teller in the next line did the same thing. With only three people left in front of him, Leonard observed the Assistant Manager, money bag in hand, go to the same door. He left it open, knelt in front of a small safe, took money from the bag, and put it in. He closed the steel door with Cottage Grove Mutual stenciled in gold on it. The manager spun the dial, dusted off the knees of his suit pants and came back into the main area. As he closed the door, Leonard could see the small safe sat next to the back door of the bank.

The teller brought him back to reality.

"Can I help you?"

Fumbling in his back pocket, Leonard said, "darn it, I left my wallet in my car, I'll be right back. Sorry."

As he left the bank, Leonard walked over to Andre and handed him the newspaper, just to piss him off.

Wind Without Rain

Leonard stood in the sunshine in front of the bank, thought a moment, then walked to the alley behind the bank. He stood there looking at the solid door with two locks and a padlocked steel bar across it. No signs of an alarm system. The bank had a lot of faith in that solid door.

A thought came to Leonard; *I'm gonna need a flatbed truck, with a winch.* He walked to the end of the alley, glanced to his right, and saw a sign, two blocks down that said ED's TOWING. It turned out Ed had a flatbed truck with a winch on it setting beside the building. Leonard looked inside the truck window, no keys in the ignition. *But you can't get everything tied up in a bow.*

Leonard walked back to the motel deep in thought. He knew what he needed next. He asked at the desk about a hardware store.

"A block off Main on Third, Cottage Hardware."

Back in the room, Leonard made a small list and called Cottage Hardware. They had what he needed.

Andre burst into their room, slamming the door. He threw the car keys, hat, sunglasses, and raincoat on Leonard's bed.

"Jesus, Leonard, do not ever approach me at a job site again, we have to remain separate. You know that."

93

"OK."

"We have to do all the planning steps. Work this out. Probably need a couple more guys. I know somebody in Astoria that could help us."

"OK."

"I have to make diagrams. We need to do surveillance, make a time chart and then —"

"OK."

"There's a lot to concentrate on. I need space, leave me alone for an—"

"OK."

Andre looked at Leonard with a scowl that would scare the shit out of most people. Leonard just smiled. Andre hated the little creep. He was going to say more, decided against it, went into the tiny bathroom, and slammed that door too.

Leonard tossed Andre's raincoat on the floor, found the car keys, and slipped out the door.

The GTO roared to life and Leonard drove to Cottage Hardware.

They had everything ready for Leonard; an acetylene torch set up, striker, welder's helmet, apron and gloves, flashlights, a fire ax, rope, and steel cable. The total came to $284.00.

The duffle bag with the cash was in the trunk under a blanket. Leonard got the necessary $284 and replaced the bag under the blanket. Two of the guys from the hardware store helped Leonard load everything into the trunk.

The next stop was the Cottage Grove Library. The Library was a Carnegie Library, one of the hundreds the robber baron had funded across the USA. Glowing white columns in front, it was the nicest building in Cottage Grove.

They too had what Leonard needed. Shown to the map section, Leonard lifted the huge county map book onto a table. He took an hour to find the location he needed. Coughing loudly, Leonard tore the appropriate section map out of the book. Stuck it in the back of his pants, with his shirt covering. He replaced the book to the shelf and left the library. Drove back to the motel.

When Leonard got back to the motel room, Andre was silent for at least five minutes, glowering, face red and getting redder. Finally:

"You took the car, no, you took my car! It's my car, not yours, not something we share. I don't want you driving it and now I don't want you even riding in it. My car!"

"Yes, I took your car. I needed to pick up some things," Leonard replied evenly.

"I don't give a shit what you needed to do. You don't take my car." Andre was furious. "What things? What did you need to pick up and what the hell did you use for money?"

"I needed things to rob the bank with. I took $284 from the duffle bag." Leonard's voice rose louder, but still under control.

"First the GTO and now you're stealing my money?" Andre's control was gone.

"Actually, our money."

"Whatever. We are weeks away from doing the bank. We need at least two more people, another getaway, better guns. And a much better plan. So, tell me Leonard, my little mastermind, when were you planning to rob the bank?"

"Tonight. You'll need another guy when you re-rob the bank 6 months from now. I'll pull the job myself tonight & be long gone by tomorrow."

It took Andre an hour to calm down. Leonard carefully laid out the plan. Andre listened, argued, cussed, shouted, and eventually accepted. It wasn't so much that he agreed, he just wanted to be rid of Leonard. If they got a few bucks out of the safe fine, but he and Leonard were done. What bothered Andre the most, really bothered him, was Leonard taking the 'leader' role.

Cottage Grove was pretty much dead after 8 pm, but Leonard and Andre waited until 1 am. Andre drove Leonard to Ed's Towing and waited in the GTO a block away, with the motor running. The black GTO looked like a panther crouched in the darkness and sounded like a wild animal ready to pounce. Leonard had to walk back and tell Andre to shut the damn thing off.

Leonard hotwired the tow truck, backed out and drove down to pick up Andre. The two of them drove in silence to the alley behind the bank. Leonard backed the truck up as close to the back door as possible. Andre pulled the steel cable from the winch, fastened the hook to the steel bar across the door.

Leonard leaped out of the idling tow truck, they had to move quickly now. He flipped on the winch switch and the cable slowly tightened, lifted off the ground in a straight horizontal line and pulled on the bar. The bar came off with a horrible screech. Next were the two locks on the door. Andre grabbed the fire ax and after several vicious blows made a hole above the locks, big enough for the winch hook to fit. The winch tore the locks off the door, and it swung open. A dog barked a couple blocks away.

The tension mounted. Someone must have heard the noise. Andre & Leonard manhandled the small safe away from the wall and got the Cottage Hardware cable wrapped around it. They secured the winch hook onto the cable and turned the winch back on. Andre & Leonard couldn't get the safe lined up in front of the door. Time was running out. They watched as the safe made its slow and clumsy way out of the bank, taking a surprisingly large chunk of the wall beside the doorway with it.

The safe made its way down the three concrete steps and jammed against a dumpster. Andre and Leonard, trying to maneuver the damn thing, swore and snarled all the way. The dumpster had to be rolled out into the alley where it slammed into Miller's Drugstore. All this made a horrendous noise, the surrounding downtown dead silent. Finally, the safe made it up onto the bed of the truck.

A circus parade would have made less racket.

With the safe securely on the flatbed, Leonard hot-wired the truck again and pulled out of the alley onto Main Street. He dropped off Andre at the GTO. Leonard and the flatbed were in the lead with Andre following. The two-car caravan headed west out of town on Gowdyville Road. After 10 miles or so, Leonard slowed to a crawl, looking for the logging road he had marked on the section map. After what seemed like an eternity to Andre, who had been watching the rearview mirror nervously, Leonard pulled off Gowdyville and onto a rough track that followed Tucker Creek.

The low-slung GTO didn't make it far. Andre got into the tow truck with Leonard and they crept along the dark, creepy, graveled road. Leonard found the spot he was looking for. The road rose on a slight ridge above the creek and Leonard backed off the road as far as he dared. They managed to push the safe off the truck then covered it with brush. Leonard pulled back on the logging road, stopped to let off Andre at the GTO, and the two headed back to Cottage Grove.

Leonard pulled the flatbed into its space at Ed's Towing. It had performed brilliantly, and the engine would be cold by the time Ed's opened in the morning. He got into the GTO with Andre and they drove back to the motel.

"We should have cut the safe open tonight," Andre snarled.

"In the dark, tired, working on rough ground? Hell, the most we would have done is start a brush fire," was Leonard's weary response.

"What if someone finds it?"

"Come on, Andre, we didn't see a car going out or coming in. We'll be back at sunrise. Nobody's gonna find it. Be lucky if we can find it again." Leonard regretted saying the last part.

The arguing only lasted 20 minutes in the motel room. They were too tired to get into it.

September 16

At first light the next morning, Andre and Leonard were at the safe. The ride up Tucker Creek logging road had been hard on the GTO and harder on Andre. The 'Goat' was dusty, dinged and scratched. It took three hours for Leonard to get the safe open. He had used an acetylene torch plenty of times at his Uncle's auto body shop in Lodi. In the time it took Leonard to get into the safe, Andre had smoked two packs of unfiltered Camels.

After the lock and its mechanism had been cut through, they used a tire iron to lever the door open.

100

There was a strong burnt odor. The heat of the acetylene burned some of the money and scorched more.

"Great, how are we going to pass these burnt bills? You should have been way more careful, Leonard."

"I was careful, and you should have taken welding in shop class. Stop your damn whining, open another pack of Camels and help me count the money." Leonard was taking the money trays out of the safe and carefully laying them on the ground.

A quick count showed $23,000, some of it singed. They did not count the burnt money.

"So, Leonard, not even as much as Sacramento."

"You're right Andre. Five grand less and nobody died, and no month-long planning delay. Planned and pulled it off in one day and best of all, only one day of your endless bullshit. Now help me push the safe off the cliff into the creek."

"I'm not doing a damn thing. You were the one that said nobody could find it. Leave it and let's go."

"Andre, we need to do this right, cover our tracks. Don't be a Dip Shit about everything."

Andre did help Leonard push the safe into the creek. As they watched the safe tumble down the cliff and into the water, Andre pulled a pistol out of this jacket pocket and shot Leonard twice in the back of the head. Once would have been enough.

"I told you not to call me that again," Andre said as he picked up the money and walked to his GTO.

September 17

Jim Olesan had fished 'his spot' on Tucker Creek forever. His Dad had taken him here when he was a little kid. Having no kids of his own, Jim had kept the spot a secret. Most people thought the water in Tucker Creek, a tributary of the south fork of the Siuslaw River, was too low for fish, but there was a giant spruce that had fallen into the river 75 years ago and it made a deep pool that trout loved. The spot was hard to get to. The trick was to watch carefully from the logging road, just before it went up the rise, for a well-hidden trail that followed the creek. Under the steep cliff was the spot.

Sliding into his mid-seventies, Jim was getting to an age where the trail was harder to navigate. Since his wife Ester passed away the year before, Jim hadn't been to Tucker Creek much. Hadn't done much of anything. After almost a year, Jim got sick & tired of his own behavior. It was time to live again. If the dear Lord thought it was time to take Ester and leave Jim, there had to be a reason.

Fishing on Tucker Creek seemed like a good way to find out what that reason was.

Jim thought he carried too damn much gear, but every time he tried to lighten his load, he left behind something he needed. He carried two poles, a creech, a tackle box with more flies & lures than he would ever need, a sack lunch and two bottles of Olympia beer. Trudging along the narrow trail, the brush and blackberry bushes tearing at his jacket, Jim stopped more often than he wanted to catch his breath and rearrange his gear. Sweating now and getting a little grumpy, Jim had to tell himself to;

Stop being a baby and get to fishing. At least the damn mosquitos are dying off.

The creek murmured in the distance. As Jim approached the pool by the fallen spruce tree, the sound of water, louder now, rushed under the spruce and against the stones on either side of the creek. It made a pleasant, rippling sound. The air was still. The sunlight filtered through the alder trees lining the pool giving everything a golden cast. There was an opening in the forest canopy over the water through which Jim could see a red tail hawk circling. He knew the effort to get here was worth it.

Jim set his 'gear and beer' down on the grass, selected the right pole, and got it set up. He was used to fishing upright, but now standing for an extended period was too much. Jim didn't mind sitting on the ground, sure it was uncomfortable, but the real problem would be getting back up.

His first cast was upstream, letting the fly carry down to the pool. Jim dropped his pole. Directly in front of him in five feet of water, was a safe with the words 'Oregon Mutual Bank of Cottage Grove,' stenciled in gold on the door.

The safe looked like it had fallen out of the sky. Jim couldn't believe it took him so long to see it. He got to his feet with a struggle and saw nearer to shore a couple of $20 bills that looked burnt.

Jim stood there staring at the safe, opened a bottle of beer and drank it trying to decide whether to start fishing or head home and call the bank. When the beer was finished, Jim picked up his gear and headed back to his truck. *Damn shame to waste a perfectly good day of fishing.*

September 19

Two days later, deputies from the Lane County Sheriff found Leonard's body halfway down the cliff.

The robbery of the Oregon Mutual Bank of Cottage Gove caused an FBI notification to all banks in Oregon, Washington, and northern California. The singed money was the main item mentioned.

13

ANDRE LEFT COTTAGE GROVE and headed south on I-5. For some reason, he hated to backtrack and was glad to turn off at Anlauf to US 99 and head west. At Drain, an odd name for such a pretty little town, Andre had a late breakfast and headed north on Oregon 38.

At Elkton, the road followed the Umpqua River. The Umpqua, bright blue, narrow and fast, wedged between the road and high hills. After Scottsburg, the river broadened, and the landscape was more open. Then on to Reedsport, getting off Oregon 38 and onto US 101, heading north, up the coast.

The Oregon coast is considered the most beautiful coastline in the world, except for the French Riviera. Since few Oregonians had been to the Riviera, and if they had, hated the French, everybody in Oregon knew which coast came in first. The Oregon State Park system was without a doubt the best in the United States. Dozens of State Parks followed Highway 101 up the Oregon Coast.

The weather was great, the scenery spectacular. Andre didn't care. His interest never went past himself. He bought a disposable camera and took a few pictures of the GTO at different beachside parks. He wanted himself in the pictures but didn't want to ask anyone to take them. Andre ended up pitching the camera in a trash bin.

Andre spent the night in Florence and the next morning, in heavy fog, he continued north. He stopped at the Sea Lion Caves. *'A bunch of barking, smelly dogs in a cave, what a rip off.'* He continued north.

Andre spent 10 days making his way up the Oregon Coast. He stayed for five nights at Salishan Lodge and later drove up the 101 a few miles, staying four days at the Inn at Spanish Head. Salishan & Spanish Head where world-class resorts; beautiful grounds, excellent views, and at Salishan one of the best golf courses in Oregon. Andre didn't take advantage of any of these amenities. He rarely left his room, except to eat and drink. He spent his days watching TV, the Phil Donahue show was his favorite. Andre paid top dollar for the biggest room available and had sumptuous lunches and dinners every day. In both establishments, he was known as a big drinker and a lousy tipper.

In those 10 days, Andre never had a thought of Leonard, nor would he ever. His brain was not hard-wired that way. He did re-think the idea of a daylight bank robbery. Not a good idea; too large of a crew required, too much risk and no time to get all the bank's money.

Should I go in at night or over a weekend? That would give me enough time to do the job right. But how could I do this? Knock a hole in the bank's wall from an adjoining building? How long would it take to find a bank with a vacant neighbor? If only there was a way to get under a bank, maybe come up through a sewer or a drain and drill or blast my way through.

Andre got antsy staying in one place too long. He again headed north on 101; thought about heading to Portland, but decided he wanted to do the entire Oregon Coast. That meant staying on 101 all the way to Astoria, and maybe going over the new Columbia River bridge he'd heard about.

This part of the drive was a wonderful trek through dark green forests, towering trees crowding the road. And ocean vistas; the bright blue Pacific and brilliant blue skies, melding at the horizon. Not that Andre paid much attention. At Neahkahnie Mountain, the roadway clung to the side of a cliff 1,000 feet above the water. It had been hacked out of the side of the mountain by convict labor. Andre pulled off at a small wayside. He got out of the GTO for a second. The view was spectacular, but the height was too much for him.

Twenty miles north, the oceanfront beach town of Seaside appealed to Andre. He liked the honky-tonk vibe and transient feel of the place. He had a 'Pronto Pup' hot dog and a 'Snow Cone' for lunch. In a rare departure against his usual nature, Andre took a ride on the Tilt-a-Whirl and the Bumper Cars. Then Cotton Candy.

Andre regretted leaving Seaside, but the Oregon Coast ended in Astoria. He checked in at the Red Lion, overlooking Astoria's West End mooring basin. His room, the biggest in the hotel, had a view of the Columbia River and the new bridge.

After a few days, Andre tired of the restaurant and bar at the Red Lion. He wanted something 'local' for a change. The Portway Tavern was just that. Within walking distance of the Red Lion, the Portway had always been a working man's joint. Since 1923, longshoreman, fisherman, cannery workers and everybody else who worked on the River, stopped at the Portway. Some stopped a lot, some never seemed to leave.

Stepping inside the Portway, it was smoky and close.

"Get me a shot of MacNaughton's and a beer back." Andre didn't so much order his drink, as demand it. The guy behind the bar looked a little frightened. Andre got that a lot. "Now, kid."

The 'kid', Joe, was just the barback. He hurried off to give the order to the bartender. Andre looked around the bar. He felt at home, liked the mix of people, and the poster behind the bar. Under a picture of a beautiful woman in a swimming suit, the text read:

NO MATTER HOW GOOD SHE LOOKS
SOME OTHER GUY IS SICK AND TIRED
OF PUTTING UP WITH HER SHIT
PORTWAY TAVERN

Andre thought - *'Well said.'*

The one shot turned into another and one more, and another after that, with an equal number of beers. By this time, The Portway was rocking. In the reflection of the back-bar mirror, Andre saw a tall, lanky guy walk in. Andre felt he knew him but couldn't get a good look through the cigarette haze. Turning around on his stool, he watched as this guy walked to the end of the bar and started talking with the barback.

"Hey Joe, how they hangin?" This was Pete's standard greeting to his friend and roommate.

"Listen, Pete, any beer you drink tonight, you are buying."

"Nice to see you too."

"I'm serious, no more free drinks. I got a lot of shit from the boss the last time. Now I can't pour drinks for anybody." Joe needed this job and wanted to move up to a bartender spot. His freeloading friend was not helping.

"OK, OK, look I got money." A cascade of dimes and nickels fell on the bar. After an inventory of all his pockets, pants, and shirt, Pete managed to get the required 75 cents for a draft beer.

"Great, when you finish that one, buy another or leave. No more taking up a stool for three hours for one beer."

"You are such a bitch. Maybe I should take my beer needs elsewhere." Pete was getting a little indignant.

"Don't forget to take your nickel tip with you."

Just then a stocky guy, not a local, with an evil-looking Fu Manchu walked up from the other end of the bar and dropped a twenty on the bar top.

"Set him up with a shot and another beer. I think I know this guy."

Joe and Pete looked at each other. This was one scary looking guy. Joe had enough of him the first time around. He gave the drink order to the bartender and went to the kitchen to get off the floor for a while.

Pete got his shot and beer. Then he remembered.

"Hey, you're right. You hung out at the Sunrise commune for a while. I'm Pete. Good to see you again." Pete couldn't remember his name.

The stranger did not offer his name or shake Pete's hand. But he did keep buying shots and beers. Pete reminisced about the Sunrise commune and explained its downfall. Then the conversation, as it always did with Pete, turned to his radical views. Pete felt the stranger was interested in his politics.

He wasn't.

"It's great to talk with someone who understands how far wrong this country has gone."

"Sure, let's get another drink and move to a table."

And that's how they spent the rest of the evening; Endless whiskey shots and beer chasers.

Pete talked and his new best friend seemed to listen.

They left at 2 am when the Portway closed.

PART FOUR
Coming Together

14

October 1

MERRI RUBBED THE PALM OF HER HAND. The burn scar bothered her at times. Reminded her of the past she left behind. She walked across campus, a wistful smile on her face.

Merri loved the Job Corps; loved the regiment. Up early. KP in the kitchen. Breakfast. Back to the room for a quick shower and on to classes. Classes on how to act. How to interact with other people. How to apply for a job (firm handshake, look them in the eye, listen, react, and do what you say.) How to eat at a restaurant. How to make your way in the world.

Then came physical exercise. Merri thought she was done with PE. But it was OK, who knew she'd be good at badminton? Another shower.

Then on to Trade Classes, a couple of days learning about each trade. What it was about, the experience and knowledge necessary. The working conditions, how much the trade paid, what the Trade Union was like. Merri was surprised how many women were interested in the traditionally male trades like Masonry or even Welding. Merri was leaning towards Bookkeeping or Dental Assistant but kept an open mind. She would have to decide when the three-week Introduction was over.

Every couple of days, there was a counselor meeting. Merri's counselor, Larry Alred, would ask Merri a few questions but mostly just listened. Then a few words of advice. Sometimes a couple of suggestions. Merri never had an adult, other than Miss Silver, listen to her before. The meetings were short.

Larry was a retired High School teacher, coach, and former Principal at Astoria High. Larry was the kind of guy that retirement did not seem to stick to. After 6 months of puttering around the house, his wife found him alphabetizing the spice rack. She told him it was time for him to find something to do – out of the house. Larry ended up being an interim superintendent at a rural school district 27 miles south-east of Astoria.

Four years there and another retirement, this time for 8 months. Again, a nudge from his wife, not so gentle this time, to seek an out of house activity. And that is how Larry ended up at the Tongue Point Job Corps. Paid for 40 hours a week, Larry put in 60 hours most weeks. Every weekday at 6:30 AM a racquetball session with another counselor, then breakfast. Great food at the Job Corps thanks to the Culinary Arts students. The calories spent at racquetball almost matched the calories consumed at breakfast.

After a full day of meetings and counseling, Larry played whatever sport was in season with one or more students. A great athlete in high school, Larry had lost a step or two with age but had gotten three or four steps smarter. Maybe craftier is a better word.

In basketball, Larry didn't run fast or jump high. But he was the guy always open for the shot, always the guy who got the rebound. Many a boastful student had his thoughts of personal athletic prowess rearranged by a match with Larry. But he was a 'good winner' and a humble one. He got that way from winning so often.

Larry had a keen interest in all his students. He knew Merri listened to his advice; absorbed it and acted on it. Larry would be a big part of Merri Sue finding her way.

After classes, at four, Merri Sue had an hour of free time. Then KP again, then dinner, a couple of social hours, a movie, usually with Penny. Then an early bedtime. Merri wasn't close to her roommate, Sammi. Which was fine with both. Merri and Penny could have roomed together. But Penny said no.

"The absolute worst thing you can do is to room with a good friend. Terrible for the friendship."

Merri took her advice.

Tom hated Job Corps. Everything about it. Hated it.

Hated getting up early. Being told what to do. Hated going to bed early. Hated being stuck in the same little hick town, Astoria, that he was born in. Now, to make it worse, he was surrounded by 425 hick kids from every other hick town across the country.

And the kids were from everywhere. Florida to Maine. New York to California. All religions. All races. In Astoria, there was exactly one Negro. Jack Black, the shoeshine guy. He had been around Astoria so long, he didn't qualify as black. More like a fixture. There were two Jewish people in Astoria, four in the entire county. At the Job Corps, there were Asian kids, Alaskan native kids (were they Eskimo? Tom didn't know for sure), Indian kids, whose people came from Bombay, and Indian kids, whose people came from Oklahoma. Asian kids whose parents spoke Japanese at home, Asian kids whose parents worked in the canneries and spoke Chinese at home.

It didn't matter to Tom. He couldn't stand any of them. Maybe the Job Corps and he weren't a good fit.

Now, he was rushing to meet his counselor, Larry. Why was there a meeting every couple of days? It all wore on him.

Larry sat behind his desk, reviewing his notes on Tom. He was a good kid in his opinion, but Tom was fighting against fitting in. Larry needed to know why. He had been a counselor for a good long time and knew with every student, a different method might be needed. Larry would use a different tack with this kid Tom.

"There is more than one way to skin a cat," Larry thought and smiled. It was a favorite expression of his father. When he first heard it as a child, it had scared Larry. In fact, he spent two nights, hiding in his closet, clutching his pet, afraid of what plans his Dad had for the cat.

Larry glanced up at the clock. Tom was late… again.

Tom burst into the door.

"You're not giving up on me, are you, Tommy? Cause I feel like you're giving up on me," Larry

121

called Tom out. He looked at his watch. "You're late, Tommy. Again."

"Sorry," Tom answered and then remembered, "Sir."

"Sorry won't do it, Tommy. Not here. Not in the real world. You cannot be late in the real world, Tommy."

"I'll try not to be late again," Tom said, "Sir."

"Try? Come on, Tommy boy, let's go for a walk."

Tom felt trouble ahead but followed. He remained quiet while Larry thought out his words.

"Tom, I want you to place a quitting notice on my desk this afternoon. The Job Corps is not right for you."

"No," Tom declared, "Sir."

"What was that?"

"I'm not giving you my notice, sir."

"I'm not giving you options here, Tom."

"And I'm not quitting, sir."

Larry stared at him. *He's not fitting in. He's late. Now he's showing balls by wanting to stay? Why the about face? Let's see what's making him tick.*

"Five o'clock, Tom. No later." Larry turned to walk away. Tom screamed at his back.

"I won't do it, sir. I'm not quitting."

Larry looked back at Tom. He saw something he had missed before.

"Why should I let you stay, Tommy boy? Let you milk the tax payer's dollars?"

The silence was thick. Tom hung his head. He mumbled, "I have nowhere to go."

"What was that, Tom?"

"I have nowhere to go."

Larry stared at a humble man in front of him and held out an inviting arm. "Come on. Let's go in. The Job Corps is perfect for you."

Slowly, things changed. It came first through sports. In school, Tom was not good enough to make the high school team but good enough for neighborhood pickup games. At Job Corps, Tom started shooting hoops with a few guys after classes. Tom had forgotten how much he liked basketball. From there on to a team on the Job Corps basketball league. Like everything else at Job Corps, it was highly regimented; referee's, scorekeepers, play clocks.

And, oddly enough, Tom liked it. It made the games better, more fun. And Tom found other sports he was interested in.

Gradually, there were changes in other parts of Tom's life. He'd chosen Commercial Carpentry as his discipline because he didn't give a damn one way or another. It turned out he was good at it. Tom liked working with his hands, with the tools, liked the smell of the sawdust, the strong sense of accomplishment seeing something he had built. Because he didn't have a high school diploma, Tom was in the GED classes. For the first time ever, Tom paid attention to his instructors. Just that, paying attention, was enough to make school understandable and if not easy, at least doable. Math became his favorite, he was good at it. Came in handy with Carpentry. As time went on, it was if a switch, deep inside Tom, was thrown. He stopped being a screw-up and became a high-functioning young man.

There was a corresponding change in Tom's personality. For the first six weeks of Tom's stay at Tongue Point, the most anyone got out of him was a scowl and a grunt. The vibe he put out was 'stay away.' Sports had helped Tom make friends with other guys, but he lacked female friends. The students at Job Corps were about evenly split, male and female. Boys being boys and girls being girls and everybody being young, there were romances and breakups and plenty of drama. The staff tried to keep a lid on things, and for the most part, they did. For Tom, romance had not crossed his mind; too busy. All that changed one day at the tennis courts.

Larry challenged Tom to a tennis match. Tom figured he would go easy on the old man; maybe let him win a few games. It was the new Tom; kind, considerate. He was in for an awakening.

Larry never moved. Firmly planted in the exact middle of the court, he returned shot after shot. Tom tried everything from going easy on the guy to trying hard to win a point to trying hard just to return a shot.

The worst part of the whole tennis thing for Tom was Larry, the bastard, never broke a sweat. He even struck up a conversation with a female student who happened to be walking by. He talked and continued the game without losing focus and continued beating Tom.

Tom asked for a timeout. He was feeling a little nauseous and it gave him a chance to check out the girl. She was tallish, with dark hair, flashing brown eyes and a figure his mother would call 'cute.' He would call her 'built.' She showed absolutely no interest what so ever in Tom. Larry and the girl, who Larry did not introduce, said goodbye.

"Another game, Tom?"

"I'd like to, but I have studying to do, thanks." It was just an excuse. His ego and body were flat worn out by the pounding he had absorbed.

Larry didn't dwell on Tom's drubbing.

Tom watched as the girl left. He didn't ask Larry about her. Later, he regretted it.

Tom sat in the cafeteria staring at his lunch plate. He was a big fan of the food at Job Corps, but today, the chili was just too hot. His friends called him a wimp for his whining. But it was just too damn hot. Spicy hot, not temperature hot. The burger & fries, however, were great, as always. They gave you so many fries, you couldn't eat them all.

"Hi, Tom," Someone said.

Tom looked up from his seat but did not recognize the young woman standing next to him. Curvaceous. Strawberry blonde. Dancing blue eyes. The kind of girl that makes men's heads turn. Just her stance told Tom that she knew it.

"I'm sorry, do I know you?"

"Sally. We had Lit together. Astoria High."

"I didn't make it to Lit often."

"I know," she said thinking of how to keep the talk going. "But it was more interesting when you came."

"I'm sorry. I should have paid more attention." Her flirtatiousness fed his ego.

"Maybe we can make up for lost time." She stared into his eyes daring him to make a move.

"Great, but I can't be late for class and I have my eye on a piece of chocolate pie. Can I get you a slice?"

"Please," she said with a dazzling smile. "I'll wait for you right here."

Tom nodded, picked up his tray, and headed to the end of the row of tables. At the end of the aisle, Tom turned right.

Merri Sue was amazed at how good the food was at Job Corps. The lunches in the cafeteria were great, but today she wasn't hungry. Maybe it was because the chili was a bit too spicy. She got up from the table, offered to bus Penny's tray as well and walked to the end of the long row of tables. She turned left to the bussing station. As she did, Merri saw a knife and fork that had slid off someone else's tray and were laying on the floor. Merri was the type of person who would stop and pick up litter whenever she saw it. She knelt at the end of the table, balanced the two trays, and retrieved the knife and fork. Dropped the fork, bent down, and got it again.

Placing the fork on top of the dirty dishes, Merri straightened up. She saw a tall body looming over her and then felt a knee hit her head.

The tall body fell across her back. Putting her arms and the trays out in front of her to break her fall, Merri hit the floor, with her face planted in the bowl of chili.

Tom was at the end of the tables, turning to get to the desserts. He saw a basketball buddy and said hi just as he rounded the end of the tables.

His knee collided with something, he couldn't tell what.

Tom started to fall. Trying to catch himself, he reached out to grab the end of the table.

His hand landed in a bowl of soup.

It and a full glass of Coke skidded off the side of the table onto an unsuspecting girl from Merri's PE class.

The soup hit the lap of the girl, the Coke hit her shoulders.

The attack of hot and cold caused the girl to vault up crashing into Tom's B-ball buddy.

The buddy, fighting to maintain his balance, deposited his fully-packed tray onto four people at the table on the other side of the aisle.

Two of these four spilled their trays as they tried to escape.

One person landed butt first on a different table causing another cascade of Coke, ice, and food. Yelling and screaming.

It was over in 10 seconds. Total casualty report: four down, 8 soaked. Collateral damage: 6 chairs and 1 table overturned. Glasses, plates, knives, and forks were all over the floor. Despite a full brigade of mops and buckets, the floor remained both sticky in some areas and slick in others. The mess on the floor seemed to call people to it causing an additional three down.

In these 10 seconds, Merri went from surprised to "damn that hurts" to pissed. Merri kicked her foot out, trying to inflict pain on her assailant. Her kick, aimed at his stomach, landed lower. Tom arched his head backward, slamming it into the underside of the table.

"Why," Tom said in a high voice, "did you do that?"

"Me? You walk like you play tennis. Are you clueless?" She stood, chili dripping from her hair.

Tom stood trying to look cool. "You're the one hiding under a table."

"At least I don't have a French fry hanging from my ear."

All coolness vanished from Tom. His face turned red as he pulled the potato from his lobe.

With that, Merri turned as if in anger and walked away, a slight smile on her face.

He's cute.

15

JOB CORP TRAINED THE MEN AND WOMEN in their ranks doing actual jobs around the campus. Today, the carpentry class would be working on their second day of the framing of an extension to the welding class that would become a storage room. The group gathered in class for direction from the instructor, then planned to go to the site to roof the storage facility. Tom sat, waiting for class to start when he looked up and saw the girl from the tennis courts enter the room. She was not a member of the carpentry group… at least not until now. Tom followed her every move until she found an empty seat on the other side of the room. She caught him watching her, and he looked away. She smiled.

The instructor discussed how they would construct the roof framework and the class headed as a group to the welding shop. As they exited the room, Tom worked his way through his classmates until he neared the girl.

"Hi. I'm Tom."

"I'm Merri. Not sure I want you this close. I don't have insurance."

The class continued to walk to the building site. Tom hesitated not knowing what to say.

"All I can say is, the French fry was tasty," Tom said.

"You wore it well, I must say," Merri said with a slight smile.

"And you, the chili. It looked great. In your hair, I mean." Now he was bumbling and feeling stupid. *Just shut up and take a breath.*

She smiled. He's a little awkward, she thought, but cute. As they reached the site, the instructor split them into teams. Merri and Tom were not working together.

"Well," Merri said, "Got to go. Safer, I suppose, if we keep our distance. Working on ladders and such."

He did not get it at first, only hearing she approved of their separation. Then he caught on and smiled.

For the next hour, he watched her as she helped lay the ceiling joists over the top plates. Even in their standard carpenter's uniform–blue coveralls and hard-tipped boots–she looked great. She worked hard too. Few women want to be carpenters–there was only one other in Tom's class–but she held her own against the men. Sitting on a top plate, she pulled planks up from her partner on the ground and laid them to rest on top of the ceiling joists. Each was twelve feet long and heavy. Later they would stand on these planks while they assembled the roof.

The roof construction itself would wait until after lunch. The class stopped at twelve and headed for the cafeteria. Tom caught up with Merri. She looked at him for a second until their eyes met.

"Can I trust you to discipline yourself while we eat, or do we need separate tables?"

Tom caught on that she was asking him to sit with her for lunch.

"On my best behavior," He swore. "I promise."

She stuck her hands deep into her coverall pockets as she smiled at Tom.

"How did you get into the carpentry class? Late?" Tom sat his tray down on the table while Merri sat across from him.

"I requested carpentry from the start but there weren't any openings. I had to wait. Someone dropped out, I heard."

"Yeah. I haven't seen Jeff in a few days."

"My grandpa was a carpenter. Grew up around it. Always loved how malleable it is."

"True. Not afraid of breaking a nail?"

"Not at all. Does my wanting to be a carpenter bother you?"

He thought he might turn her off. It was not his intent.

"I was thinking earlier you look good in coveralls."

"Just good?"

"Well, I don't want you to get a big head."

"Noted." She liked him, but experience told her to keep her guard up. He was cute and engaging. Easy to get along with. The longer they talked, the lower the guard went. They ate and smiled. Tom avoided any clumsy moves and Merri buried her critical thoughts of men.

It was October and the chill of the Columbia River breeze forced the cafeteria's heater next to Merri to kick in. The sweater she had on under her coveralls was too hot. Merri unzipped it as far as it would go. Tom noticed.

"Listen," he said, "On our free time, why don't we have dinner or a movie?"

"I'd like that. Though lunch has gone well, maybe a movie would be safer."

Tom accepted the jab with a nod of his head.

"Saturday night. The movie starts at seven."

"I'd love it."

16

WITH HER LEGS PROPPED UP to support a magazine, Sammi lay on top of her bed. A strategically placed pillow kept the headboard bearable. She flipped through Cosmopolitan magazine, stopping at an article about Goldie Hawn. Large, four-inch-round eyeglasses tinted rose dominated Goldie's face. The glasses were all the rage. Good enough for Goldie Hawn. Good enough for Sammi.

Merri Sue paced between the small dresser with its attached mirror and the bathroom.

"Merri, please."

"What?"

"I'm trying to read."

"I'm not talking."

"You're wearing the shag off the carpet."

Merri stopped and looked at the stringy gold floor covering. A dark worn path looped around their beds and into the restroom.

"That might not be a bad thing, Sammi."

"My point is, you're zipping back and forth. Try to relax. It's just a movie." Sammi smiled. Merri obviously liked this guy Tom. Merri never worked this hard getting ready.

"I'm relaxed," She defended herself. "I just want to feel good about myself."

"What you want is to look good for Tom."

"Well, maybe a little."

"Maybe a lot. You look great."

Merri's bellbottom jeans covered her heeled, open-toed shoes and were immaculately pressed. A peasant blouse with three-quarter-length sleeves finished the look.

"You think so?"

"I know so. Relax. Come here." Sammi patted the bed inviting Merri Sue to sit. Merri still had a lot to do but sat.

Sammi stared at her for a second.

"You like him, don't you?"

"I guess. I don't want to. I mean, men are men, right? It never works out well for me."

"Can't find the right one if you don't go shopping."

"He is cute, right?"

"Right. What's more important is your face lights up when you talk about him."

"Really?" It embarrassed Merri that her feelings for Tom had slipped out. Sammi saw something that Merri wasn't ready to accept. Her affection for Tom scared Merri.

"Maybe I'll stay in tonight. We can do something together."

"You'll do no such thing. I won't help you ruin your life. Get out there. Make things happen."

"I guess."

The setting sun edged the dark clouds with a light blue. Tom looked skyward. Rain would not be unusual for Astoria, but Tom hoped for a clear night. He wanted everything to go well. He puffed into his cupped hand checking his breath and knocked on Merri's door. No one answered. He heard muffled voices inside and waited.

Finally, the door opened.

"Hi. I'm Sammi." She offered her hand for a shake.

"Tom." He looked past her shoulder for Merri.

"She'll be ready in a sec. Come in."

Two beds took up most of the efficiency room. Tom sat at the end of one. Sammi plopped down next to him. Tom felt she was checking him out. She was.

"So, where you from?"

The grilling started.

"Right here in Astoria."

"Merri tells me you're in carpentry with her."

"That's right." He turned the questioning around. "And you?"

"Medical Imaging."

An awkward silence ensued. Merri broke it as she entered the room. Tom stood and stared at the stunning woman in front of him. Her amber eyes and white smile radiated.

He smiled.

"You two having a good conversation?" Merri questioned.

"Ah," Tom said, "You came just in time."

Merri glanced Sammi's way.

"I apologize for my EX-roommate putting you through fifty questions."

Sammi smiled.

"Not a problem. We should get going though."

Merri donned her coat as Tom opened the door. Merri turned to Sammi with a large grin. Sammi held up the entwined first two fingers of her right hand.

Good luck.

Tom turned up the collar of his jacket and sank his hands deep in his pocket for warmth. Merri slid her hand around his arm. All the warmth she needed came from Tom. They headed across the street that ran through Job Corps to a warehouse-sized building. It housed two restaurants that gave Sammi and the other Hospitality group practice learning their craft. Behind the eateries, the movie theater offered weekend, second-run movies. Tonight, *Wait Until Dark* was playing. A safe movie for date night, Tom thought. Not a romance. *Too much, too fast?* Not a western. *Too much killing and blood?* And, Audrey Hepburn. Perfect.

They decided on a bite to eat before the show and headed for The Bistro. Tom ordered a hamburger with fries. Merri got a salad with thousand island dressing. Tom suggested they share a malt.

"You pick the flavor," Merri said.

When the food arrived, Merri stared at Tom's French fries until he noticed.

"What?"

"Daring to order fries after the cafeteria incident the other day."

"I thought we agreed that day never happened?"

Merri reached out, placed her warm hand on his, and said,

"But I'm glad it did."

"Good point." Tom smiled.

The conversation was easy. They continued to touch hands. Neither worried that the movie had started.

Eventually, Tom looked around. They were sitting in an empty restaurant, the staff waiting for them to leave.

Merri never wanted the night to end.

"I guess we missed the movie," Merri giggled. Tom helped her with her coat. As they stepped outside, rain pounded the pavement. Merri screeched as they ran across the road to student housing. As they approached Merri's room, Tom pulled her aside, under the eaves of another building. He placed her back against the wall and stared into her eyes. And she in his. He cocked his head, a kiss inevitable.

"You two having a good night?" Larry stood behind them. Though unavoidable, Job Corps discouraged fraternizing amongst the students.

Tom and Merri straightened up. Busted.

Embarrassed, they stood silent.

Larry let the awkwardness last a few seconds.

"Tom. Might I have a word with you?"

Tom glanced at Merri. He had no choice.

"Of course. I'll see you tomorrow," he said to Merri.

Larry threw his rain-drenched arm around Tom's shoulder and walked him away.

Tom expected a lecture.

"Nice girl. Hard worker. Loyal. Good heart."

Tom was surprised.

"Yes, sir."

"Let's get out of this rain."

17

AND SO, IT BEGAN. Staying mostly under the radar, Merri & Tom became an item. During the day, they were strictly classmates (although they did have lunch together every day, using Penny as a beard.) The nights were different. As soon as their Job Corps duties ended, Tom and Merri were together. They enjoyed the on-site movies, the library, and long walks through the campus. Anything to be together.

As the relationship grew, sometimes Merri's roommate, Sammi, left the room for a couple of hours. Merri and Tom never went to his room. Merri trusted him but she refused to be 'locker room' gossip among the guys. No way.

Larry knew about their relationship but dealt with it in a detached sort of way. It came up a couple times in Tom's counseling sessions.

"Tom, what I'm telling you is that the Job Corps has a firm policy against classmates dating." Larry stated the official policy.

"I know, I know . . . you told me before."

"And I'm also telling you," Larry said off the record, "that this girl is one in a million. You'd be crazy to stop seeing Merri. Do you understand, Tom?"

"Yeah . . . I guess. I don't want to get her in trouble with Job Corps."

"Or anything else," Larry added.

"Right, or anything else," Tom agreed.

"Just keep it low key on the base, no hand holding, nothing 'lovey-dovey' and you'll be all right." Larry had said his piece.

"I will keep it low key," Tom repeated. Even though he and Merri planned a rendezvous in Merri's room that night.

"One last thing, this is a chance of a lifetime Tom. Don't screw it up."

"I won't."

What is there to say about happiness? So much easier to describe anger or conflict. However, you put it, they had it. Tom and Merri were happy. This relationship was the last missing piece to the 'New' Tom. He now had someone and something to protect, to build upon. Big plans for them both. Marriage not in the picture yet. Way too early. They hadn't even talked about it, but they both thought about it. Tom in sort of a grand life plan he envisioned and for Merri a faraway dream.

Tom idolized Merri. In his eyes, she was perfect. Merri made a few changes in Tom. Got him to get a decent haircut. He and his roommate had been cutting their own hair to save money. Got him to wear nicer and more appropriate clothes. Suggested books he might read. Just a few (well, more than a few) minor changes.

Everything Merri suggested, Tom did.

As time passed, Tom and Merri took advantage of 'Off Campus' passes. Both did well in their classes and Job Corps rewarded them. They looked forward to their nights out in downtown Astoria. The banana split at the counter at Lawson Drug, a favorite for them. One time, they splurged big time and went to

Sunset Empire Room for a steak dinner. The dark, bustling restaurant across from the Mill Pond was a serious date night. Seated, Cokes ordered, and menus given, Merri and Tom realized steak was out of the question. They couldn't afford one steak dinner, much less two. Both ordered a hamburger, plain, no soup, no salad. They had a great time and it became a favorite memory for Tom and Merri.

On another night after a so-so movie at the Liberty Theater, they bumped into Tom's parents. Almost walked right by them in the crosswalk. Fred Thompson and his wife Marjorie didn't recognize the handsome young man with the pretty woman on his arm. What happened to their son? Was this really him? Introductions were made as the 'Walk' sign turned to 'Don't Walk.' Marjorie couldn't stop staring at Tom. Fred tried not to stare at the great looking young woman.

Tom's parents insisted they go to the Fiesta Club restaurant for coffee and dessert. Fred and Marjorie were amazed at the young adult couple sitting in the booth across from them. These two were not kids. Tom and Merri knew how to hold up their end of an adult conversation. Knew how to order and act in a restaurant.

The other thing, very evident, was these two were in love.

Tom excused himself to go to the restroom. On the way back, he stopped the waiter and asked for and paid the check.

"Merri, we need to get going. We can just make the last bus," Tom said as he got back to the table. "Mom, Dad, great to see you both."

"Tom, your Mother and I can drive you back."

"Thanks, Dad, but we'll take the bus. Nice to have a bit of alone time. And I got the check."

Fred and Marjorie looked at each other in amazement as Tom and Merri hurried to the bus.

Now they knew why Tom missed a few Sunday dinners. They noticed other changes but had not seen this. Their son was a man now and in love.

They liked the new Tom and were proud.

And totally amazed.

The dense moisture in the air changed to grape-sized drops of rain pounding on the awning in front of Loop Jacobsen Jewelers. Tom and Merri ducked into the alcove under the awning hoping the rain would let up soon. They needed to catch the bus back to Job Corps. Merri giggled as she shook off her coat.

"I had a great time with your parents tonight," she said. "They're special."

Tom looked into her eyes.

"You're special."

She smiled, and they hugged, Merri facing the display window of the jewelry store. A worker collected the various pieces of rings and necklaces and watches and a bright sparkle caught her eye.

"Tom, look."

Merri pointed to an engagement ring, large and expensive, that flamed with brilliance next to a small Help Wanted sign.

"It's beautiful," he admitted.

"Someday," she mumbled, her mind wandering to a dream of a future. "If I ever find the right man," she teased as she smiled at Tom.

"The right man? Ouch."

Merri giggled.

"Don't you worry. I've found him." She stretched up into his arms and kissed him.

"Good answer. Look, we need to get going."

"Your right. We'll be late."

Tom looked over his shoulder at the display window as the worker collected the ring. *Someday,* he thought.

18

THE THOMPSONS INVITED THEIR SON and Merri Sue to Sunday dinner, a big deal for all concerned. It would be nice for the parents to see their son, but Marjorie needed to know the young woman so important to Tom. Fred reminded himself not to comment on Merri's good looks. A previous cold stare from Marjorie told him he mentioned this once too often.

Saturday before the dinner, Marjorie spent the entire day cleaning. The operating rooms at Columbia Memorial Hospital weren't as clean as the Thompson household by the time she finished. The pending dinner was important to her.

Fred hid out in his 'workshop' in the garage the entire day.

Generally, Sunday was church day for the Thompsons. Bible study at 10, church service at 11

(Marjorie sang in the choir) and a coffee klatch following. Home about 1, Tom Sr would stretch out on the couch and doze through whatever sporting event was on TV. Marjorie would work in the yard or maybe take a nap herself, then make Sunday dinner.

But on this Sunday, Marjorie skipped bible study. Instead, she stayed home and made dough for the dinner rolls. She set the dining room with her best lace tablecloth, the good china, crystal glassware, and her Mother's silver service.

Fred's contribution was to make an unholy mess in the living room with the Sunday Oregonian newspaper.

"Fred, pick up that paper right now. And take your coffee cup and ashtray into the kitchen."

Fred suggested it might be better if he spent the whole day in the garage.

Marjorie agreed. "If you can't help, get out of the way."

On the silent ride to the church, Marjorie imagined Sunday dinner in her mind. The first course would be tomato aspic, a Jell-O-like concoction, using tomato juice instead of water, with bay shrimp and celery. For serving, Marjorie topped it with mayonnaise. An unusual dish, and one that frightened small children.

The main dish would be fried chicken, Marge considered ham, but chicken seemed more welcoming. Mashed potatoes, corn, dinner rolls, and a green salad finished out the main course with tea and homemade lemon bars as dessert.

At church, Marjorie sang in the choir as Fred nodded off in the pew.

Dinner was set for 5. As if Merri wasn't nervous enough, Tom's grandparents were coming. Merri couldn't decide which dress to wear, she only had two. In the end, she borrowed one of Sammi's. Merri had Tom stop and get his mother flowers on the way.

As they walked up to the Thompson's front door, Merri noticed the manicured small front yard. Not a fallen Autumn leaf was left. Trees were pruned. Flower beds groomed. Obviously, a cared-for yard. Tom wanted to barge right in, but Merri made him knock first. His father opened the door.

Fred wore a 'Modern Cocktail Apron' with illustrations and recipes for '24 Cocktails' printed on it. It was quite a sight.

Fred wore the apron over the white shirt and dark slacks left over from church. He loosened his tie. Marjorie bustled out of the swinging kitchen door. She too wore the dress from church. She had changed when she got home and only put the dress back on 15 minutes ago after she fixed her hair and makeup.

Marjorie graciously accepted the flowers from Tom, knowing it was Merri's idea.

Merri was glad she had dressed up.

"Well kids, what shall we drink?"

"Thanks, Dad. I guess water for Merri and me."

"Come on, water? Let's get adventurous! I know, I'll make us Apple Blossoms."

"Can't Dad. Job Corps doesn't allow drugs or alcohol."

"Oh yeah, right." Fred couldn't help thinking how much money he would have saved on car insurance if Tom had taken a temperance pledge in high school before the two DUI's.

They all sat down to chat and catch up. Merri ate a few of the cocktail peanuts strategically placed in small dishes around the room. After a few minutes, Marg got up, saying she needed to do a few things in the kitchen. Merri followed her through the swinging door.

"I've got to get this dinner going or we won't eat till midnight. Merri, if you want to sit at the table and keep me company, that would be great.

"Dear, what I do with fried chicken is mix up flour, salt, pepper in a brown paper bag and then add the chicken parts and shake it like crazy."

Merri would have added smoked paprika to the flour mixture, but she kept that to herself.

"Then, and here's the secret, I take the chicken pieces out of the bag, put them on a plate and into the fridge for 20 minutes."

Merri nodded in agreement. It was how her Mother taught her. The time in the fridge made the coating stick to the chicken creating extra-crispy skin.

"Then I fry it up in Crisco in my Mother's cast iron pot."

Merri would have used lard, but Crisco would work. And a well-used and seasoned cast iron pot was better than the cheap aluminum pot Merri and her Mom used.

As Marjorie busied herself, Merri noticed the salad fixings setting on the table. Without asking, she washed all the produce, found a cutting board, and sliced the carrots, celery, shallots, and tomatoes.

Marg pointed to the cupboard where the new 'Salad Spinner' sat. Merri had never seen such a thing.

"It's for washing the lettuce. My in-laws gave it to me last year for Christmas. A strange gift, but it works great." Marge was right, it did work great.

Next, Merri washed and peeled potatoes and set them in a pot of cold, salted water on the stove.

Tom's grandparents arrived, his grandfather tall, holding his briar pipe, dressed in his Sunday best cardigan and tie. His grandmother, short, almost tiny but round. After the introductions, she followed the women into the kitchen. The grandfather joined the men in the living room in front of the TV.

Tom's grandmother, Alice, handed Marjorie a can of black olives completing Sunday dinner protocol. She always brought olives and only olives. Marjorie did the cooking.

Alice and Merri hit it off right away. Alice saw in Merri the same beautiful, confident young woman she was at the same age.

To Merri, Alice's husband Wayne seemed the tall, silent type and Alice, the small, vivacious type. And that worked fine for Merri. She found out more of the Thompson family from Alice in 10 minutes than she pried out of Tom since they met.

The potatoes done, Marge asked Merri to mash them.

"Here's the butter and the cream, dear. Sometimes I use butter, sometimes cream. You decide."

Merri used both. Alice noticed, smiled, and nodded in agreement. The whole point of mashed potatoes was excess.

Dinner went well. Merri got the men and Alice to the table and helped Marge bring out the food. Hands

156

held, heads bowed, and grace said. Something new for Merri. Everyone enjoyed the food and complemented Marjorie, who shared the credit with Merri.

The 'Tomato Aspic with Bay Shrimp' challenged Merri, but she dutifully took a bite and then another. And she liked it. Hard to believe a savory, seafood Jell-O dish would taste good.

Years later, Merri would make this dish for her kids and grandkids at every holiday dinner. And they all hated it. At first.

Tom and Fred insisted on clearing the table which of course made a bigger mess. The kitchen went from crowded with pots and pans to a disaster zone of pots, pans, plates, serving plates, utensils, and glasses. Wayne showed the good sense to sit in the living room, smoking his pipe.

"All men out of the kitchen. You too, Alice." Marge said this in a loud enough voice to cause an immediate exodus. Then she and Merri went to work. Everything stacked appropriately, leftovers into the refrigerator, all the pans, dishes, utensils, and glasses hand washed, dried, and put away.

Fred gave Marge a dishwasher last Christmas. Poor Marge couldn't get a break from the Thompson family on Xmas gifts. And she didn't think the dishwasher did all that great of a job. For the good china and glasses, she would rather do it herself.

Coffee, tea, and lemon bars were served and shortly after, Tom's grandparents left. It turned out they were Bonanza fans and didn't want to miss the next episode. Like his parents, Fred faithfully watched Bonanza every week. He and Tom headed for the living room and the TV.

Merri and Marge retreated to the kitchen and over a cup of tea, in the glow of a job well done, a bond struck. Woman to woman, members of an extended tribe. Merri learned more about the Thompson family and more importantly about Thompson men.

That bond between these two women lasted until Marjorie's death.

19

November 18

PENNY HAD CAUGHT MERRI SUE as they walked back to their rooms after class.

"Hey, Merri do you want to go to the movie? True Grit's showing. It's the last night."

"Gee I'd like to, but Tom and I went last night. We're going into town for a burger at Arctic Circle. Do you want to come with us?"

And there it was... again. Penny couldn't get time alone with Merri. Not since Tom came on the scene. What little time she got was always Merri, Tom and the 3rd wheel, Penny.

"That's alright, Merri, we can get together some other time."

That other time wouldn't be for a week or two. And it would be a hurried cup of coffee at best, rushed because Merri and Tom had to go or do something. They always invited Penny along and she went at first, but they didn't really need her. They were just being polite. Merri and Tom were in love and there wasn't room for anybody else.

Tom was nice enough and Penny was happy for her friend. But she missed Merri. Having a good friend to talk with and share all the things going in their lives. Now that was gone.

Lunch with Merri used to be the favorite part of the day for Penny. Gossip, laughter, nothing serious; that would come later in the day, after classes. They would go over the day and plan for the next and beyond. Big plans, where they would go in their lives and what they could achieve.

Now at lunch, Penny was included just so Tom and Merri wouldn't seem like a romantic couple. As if everybody didn't already know. Penny thought she had made a mistake not rooming with Merri. It seemed like a good idea. Better for the friendship. But now it was Sammi that Merri would confide in after lights out.

Penny wasn't jealous of Tom or of his relationship with Merri. Although she couldn't come up with a better name for her feelings. She was happy Merri had found a nice guy. But Penny hadn't found her own nice guy.

Penny was back at square one. Always the 'wallflower' trying to fit in, to be a part of a group, to have a boyfriend.

And failing at it all.

And hating it.

20

FRANK VAN WINKLE STARED through the magnifying goggles at the pocket watch stretched out on the workbench, its intricate insides exposed. A goose-necked desk lamp, its green-glass shade hovering inches from the timepiece, cast bare white light on the moving parts. He was the third generation Van Winkle to work in the store. His father, Rip, walked behind him as he finished putting out the last felt-lined tray of jewelry to the display windows.

Frank was a gentle, soft-spoken man. Gray at the temples, his short stubby flat top stood up above the goggles with the help of a generous application of butch wax. The overalls were old and frayed. Martha, his wife, had threatened many times to throw them out, but he insisted they were just fine as they were. The elder Van Winkle wore a business suit, dark, with a white dress shirt, and a thin black tie. His eyes were not what they used to be, and he had succumbed to the reality that his repair days were over. Now he waited on customers while his son did repairs.

The hand-built wood front door hit a hanging bell as it opened announcing Tom's entrance. He walked in confidently as taught at Job Corps. Glass countertops lined both sides of the store, the right one continuing ninety degrees into the room separating the front of the store from the back. Through a broad archway, Frank's work area flanked the left side. Centered on the back wall was a five-foot-tall floor safe, its door ajar.

Rip approached.

"How may I help you?" The older Van Winkle asked.

"I saw your sign in the window. I want to apply, sir."

Tom shook hands firmly with him.

"I'm Rip Van Winkle." He saw it on Tom's face. The same look he always got. "Real name is Jonathan, but kids are cruel. 'Rip' stuck to this day. Even Mom, rest her soul, called me Rip."

Mr. Van Winkle was not impressed with the young man. *Sure, he's neat, his shirt and trousers pressed, and courteous, but where's the suit?*

"I'm Tom Thompson… and my father always said, 'You can call me anything but late for dinner,' But I will call you Mr. Van Winkle, sir."

Rip called out to his son, "I believe you forgot to take down the Help Wanted sign. I am sorry, Tom, but the position is filled." It was not true, but Rip would wait for a more suited applicant.

"I see," Tom said, disappointment showing. "Can I leave my name and number? In case things don't work out for your new hire?"

"Of course," Rip said appeasing him. "Let me grab you a pencil and paper."

Tom wrote the information. "The number is for Job Corps. You can leave a message there."

Rip started to cut the conversation short when his son came out from the work area. Frank pushed up his goggles to his forehead.

"Did you say Job Corps, young man?"

"Yes. Why?"

"Great thing they are trying to do. My friend, Larry Alred, works over there. You know him?"

"Yes, he's my counselor." Tom felt a connection. "He's helped me a lot."

"We went to school together. Terrible tennis player, but a good man."

"I don't know. He seems to run me all over the court."

Frank glanced at his father as he continued to take over the conversation.

"The key with Larry is to overplay his forehand and attack his backhand. He cannot handle it."

Tom shook Frank's hand as he approached. "Thank you for the advice. I'll be on my way. It was great speaking with you."

"Not so fast, son. Does Larry know you are applying for a job?"

"Yes. Weekends only though. I'm not through with Job Corps yet."

"Uh huh. Wait a second."

Frank walked past his father, reached over the display of watches, and grabbed a heavy, black telephone, its cord tangled like spaghetti. He dialed zero on the rotary dial.

"Yes, would you connect me to Larry Alred at the Job Corps out at Tongue Point? Thank you." After a pause, "Larry. Frank Van Winkle. How have you been?" Pause. "I would love a game, but I was hoping for more of a challenge. Listen, I have a young man," Frank glanced at the information Tom had written, "Tom Thompson, here applying for a job on the weekends." Pause. "I see. That is all I need to hear. Look forward to Sunday. About Noon?" Pause. "See you then."

Frank cradled the handset on the phone base and looked to Tom.

"The job is yours, Tom."

"That is great. When should I start?"

"What are your plans today?"

"I'm free all afternoon."

"Good. Let's take care of some paperwork and then I will turn you over to my father.

"Come on," Frank said, "Let's get you settled in."

Tom turned to Frank's father. "It was a pleasure meeting you. I'm looking forward to working for you, Mr. Van Winkle."

"Welcome aboard. Please call me Rip."

"Rip it is, then."

Tom took a quick glance at the window that displayed the engagement ring Merri Sue loved, then followed Frank into the back room.

21

November 21

SALLY SAT DOWN NEXT TO PENNY in the cafeteria. They exchanged smiles. Sally had conjured up a plan and Penny was a big part of it.

"Hi," Sally said.

Penny smiled but said nothing.

Sally ate a fry and took a bite of her BLT before trying again to start a conversation. She stared across the cafeteria at Tom who was sitting with Merri Sue. They shared many smiles Sally noticed. "So, you and Merri are good friends?"

"That's right."

"Nice girl," Sally said to build trust.

"Yes, she is my best friend here at JC."

"She seems to be enjoying her company today." Sally nodded her head in Tom's direction. Penny turned but looked uninterested.

"Yeah, but it's none of my business."

"You're right. It's just that Tom and I had a thing going in school. Pretty hot, actually."

"Really? Things seem to have changed for Tom now."

"I don't know about that, but I do know he came on to me yesterday."

"Oh yeah? And how's that working out for you?" Penny said glancing back at Merri Sue and Tom.

"We'll see," Sally said as she rose, ignoring her half-eaten sandwich.

Penny watched as Sally fluffed her hair, took a deep breath, and started towards Tom. Another deep breath as she neared the table.

"Hi, Tom," Sally said in a friendly tone. "Good to see you… again."

Tom was caught off guard. He did not remember her name. Merri sensed Tom's awkwardness, felt something was wrong, and stood. She stuck out her hand in Sally's direction.

"Hi. I'm Merri. And you would be?"

Sally ignored Merri.

"After yesterday, Tom, I thought I'd come by to say hi."

Tom, taken aback, glanced at Merri and saw anger. He realized he was standing in quicksand with no one there to throw him a rope.

Merri's defenses kicked in. Her walls went up. She turned to Tom.

"What happened yesterday, Tom?"

"Nothing, Merri. We—" Sally cut him off before he could explain.

"We spent some time together," Sally said not lying but not painting a fair picture either. She looked into Tom's eyes. It was all Merri's vulnerability could handle.

"I'm outta here," she declared as she retreated toward the exit.

"Merri, wait," Tom called out, but she continued walking away.

"Forget her, Tom. She'll be okay. Let's sit and talk."

"I have nothing to talk to you about. Stay out of my affairs. You hear?"

She shrugged her shoulders posing an innocent face.

Tom looked at Merri walking away. He glanced at the clock hanging on the cafeteria wall. Lunch hour was over. No time to fix things now, but they would spend the afternoon in Carpentry workshop together.

No telling how that's going to go.

22

November 21

MEMBERS OF THE CARPENTRY GROUP met at the welding shop worksite. Fortunately for Tom, Merri Sue would be there. Unfortunately for Merri Sue, she would have to show up. It would be awkward.

Tom showed up first. He took to the roof to lay sheathing with a classmate, Edgar. They hung out awaiting the rest of the class. For Tom, that only meant Merri. He did not wait long. She rounded the corner of the welding shop and approached the new construction. By habit, she looked up at the project, proud of what they were accomplishing, but saw Tom there. Her eyes dropped to the ground floor. Her stomach churned.

Tom started to say something, but she avoided his eyes. *This might be a long afternoon.*

As the team got started, Merri and Ralph lifted a four by eight sheathing up to the roof where Edgar and Tom pulled it up. Tom tried to smile at Merri, but her eyes avoided him. Edgar secured the board while Tom measured for a partial piece needed.

"Four by five and a half," he said. Merri never looked up but helped Ralph lay a full sheet on the sawhorses. She measured, picked up a Skill saw, and while Ralph held the needed piece, she made her cut.

Tom decided on levity.

"Don't have all day up here," he said.

Finally, Merri looked up at him.

"You seem to have plenty of time when you need it."

Tom was lost. *What did that mean?*

Merri wasn't done. She had too much pent up inside her.

"OK, who is this Sally chick and what does she mean to you? Tell me now and tell me the truth."

"I don't have a clue what you are talking about, Merri. I don't know her. Today was only the second time I've seen her."

The instructor coming over. Tom focused on his work.

"We have a problem here?"

"No, sir," Tom said.

"Only one," mumbled Merri.

"What was that?"

"Nothing, sir. No problem."

"Good. Let's get back to work." The instructor glanced up at Tom. He refocused on the sheathing.

Ralph said in a low voice, "What's going on? You're bringing me into this."

"Sorry," Merri replied. "Tom is a shit is all." She thought for a second. "Men!"

"So, I'm included in that list?"

Merri smiled, though her anger at Tom still simmered inside her.

"Of course, not," She said. "At least, not yet."

Ralph helped Merri lift a sheathing to the roof.

"Good. I was uncomfortable being so close with a Skill saw in your hands. Never seen you angry before."

"He flirts with another woman. Saw it with my own eyes. Same old story."

"Doesn't sound like Tom. You sure?"

She glanced up at Tom as he placed the sheathing. "Doesn't matter anymore."

Cold personalities were everywhere the rest of the afternoon. At four o'clock, Merri left quickly. Ralph lagged to talk to Tom.

"What did you do? She's pissed."

"I have no idea. One minute we have something going. The next, this. You tell me cuz I haven't a clue."

"She said she caught you flirting with another woman."

"What? No way."

"That's what she said."

Where did that come from? Sally!

"It was an old classmate from high school. Don't even know her name."

"She seems sensitive for a reason. Go easy on her."

Tom felt frustrated by it all.

"Maybe I need to focus on Job Corps."

"Can't catch a fish if you don't throw out a line."

"Seriously? That's the best ya got?"

"You have to pay to get the good ones."

"Good thing I'm broke."

They both smiled but Tom was not giving up on Merri. He'd confront her later and clear things up.

Penny lay on her bed, studying. The front door burst open and Merri tossed herself face down on the other bed.

"What's going on?" Penny sat up on the edge of the bed. Merri said nothing, her face buried in the pillow. "Okay. None of my business but if you need to talk, I'm here for you."

Merri sat up, turning to look at Penny. Her eyes red. Her arms crossed over her chest.

"I'm pissed."

Penny had never seen her friend so mad. "Pissed at who?"

"I'm pissed at Tom and every other man I've ever known"

"What do you mean, Merri?"

"All my life, men promised me this. Promised me that. It's all hot air. They're all full of shit."

"Not going to argue with you there. But your expectations are a bit high. They're only this side of Cro-Magnon."

Penny caught a slight smile at the corner of Merri's mouth. She stood and sat next to Merri, putting a comforting hand on Merri's shoulder.

"What did Tom do?"

"We were having lunch together. Everything was going fine. Then, someone named Sally comes over and starts flirting with Tom. Right in front of me."

"And Tom did what?"

"Well, I don't know. She had her arm around him and gave him THAT look."

"So far, the only guilty party is her. She came over. She put her arm around him. She looked at him."

Merri thought about it a moment.

"I guess you're right. Oh, I'm such a mess."

"Wait. I remember something she said." Penny thought a moment longer. "Tom came on to her yesterday. Maybe your gut is telling you something after all."

Tom headed for Merri's room. Confusion fogged his mind. *Why am I in trouble here? What did I do wrong? In the legal system, you're innocent until proven guilty. Not with women!*

Tom crossed the road to the cafeteria and entered the squeaking door. He passed the buffet line which was closed. Only shiny stainless steel remained. And a vase of flowers at the end for decoration. Tom caught the eye of a student working in the kitchen. Tom pointed to the flowers.

"I need these more than you do," he said.

The student cupped his hand over his eyes as if saying 'I see nothing.'

Tom grabbed the vase and continued to Merri's. He was not sure what he would say. Hopefully, the flowers would help though. He rapped on the door. It took forever for a response but then he heard footsteps. The door opened. It was Merri's roommate, Sammi.

She remained silent as she stared at Tom.

"Is Merri here? I need to speak to her."

"She's not here," Sammi said, though she motioned with her eyes that Merri was behind the door. "Try the tennis courts."

"Sammi, go for a walk. Merri and I need to talk."

Sammi scrambled outside around a man in control. Tom closed the door behind him. Merri stared at him, eyes wet with tears. She tried to wipe them dry.

"Merri, whatever you think is going on, you're wrong. I didn't —"

"You came here to tell me I'm wrong? Great start. How's this for an ending?" She grabbed the flowers out of the vase and broke the stems in half. She held them in the air and released them to the floor. "That's all I have to say. You can take them and stick it.

But Merri, I —"

"But nothing. Just leave… leave!"

Tom stood in silence for a second, then turned for the door.

"Merri, I don't know what you are talking about. I only know what was starting between us is important to me.

Merri had heard that before. She tossed the flower vase at him.

"Take your vase back to the cafeteria. It means something to them."

Tom looked at the vase. Looked at her. Left the room.

PART FIVE
Crossroads

23

BILL SLID HIS RIGHT HAND through his red curly hair, his try at grooming, then wiped it on his jeans. He caught Joe watching him, so he licked a pinky finger and ran it over an eyebrow. He smiled at Joe and they both laughed. They were on their way to the basement where Peter, Bill, and Joe were squatting. Pete said he had great news. He did not elaborate. The guys trespassed the backyard of the three-story Victorian to its basement door. They passed by a thin, rectangular window meant to let light into the basement, but a heavy piece of cardboard had replaced the window. The guys did not want their presence known. Bill looked around and, seeing no one, threw his shoulder at the door as he turned the doorknob. Most of the ground in Astoria was making a slow march to the river. Foundation problems for the 100-year-old home made the doors not fit correctly. A massive crack in the cement next to the entrance was proof of it; a small price to pay for free rent.

As the duo entered the basement, Joe noted a stranger in their midst. *Damn it's the weird guy from the bar.*

Peter turned to greet his buddies.

"Guys." His voice upbeat, he turned to the stranger. "This is a new friend of mine. I believe he can help us."

The men exchanged pleasantries, but Peter did not introduce the unknown man by name.

"I'm sorry. I didn't get your name." Bill was uneasy with the stranger.

Peter jumped in to control the discussion. "That's because he wants to help us but wants no notoriety for it. I'll explain in a minute. Sit, guys."

The men scrambled to find a seat. Bill sat in a bent-leg beach chair while Joe chose a camping ice chest; old but still able to support his ample girth. The stranger sat on Bill's bed pad which was not sitting well with Bill.

Peter remained standing to sell his thoughts to the gang.

"Remember last weekend we discussed needing to make a large impact to create change in our society? Well, you'll find our friend's talent interesting."

"Help us with what, Peter?"

Peter pointed Joe's way as if he had an epiphany. "Exactly!" Peter exclaimed and then lost his direction. He stood in silence for a second until his thoughts refocused. "Mr.—" he hesitated, "X has significant skills we need to make our statement." Mr. X nodded his head as he scanned the guys and acknowledged his introduction.

"I'm not with you, man," Joe admitted, and Bill nodded agreement.

Bill stretched to his left and grabbed a cigar box mixed with the rubble that covered the floor. He rolled a joint with little concern for Mr. X's presence. Bill licked the paper, sealed it, and lit it. Taking a long hit, he savored it for a moment and passed it to Joe. Bill thought to himself he had enjoyed better, but any joint beat a day without one. Joe offered the doobie to Mr. X who hesitated before passing it to Peter without taking a hit. Bill was not impressed.

Peter continued. "I've been thinking. If we want recognition, people need to know who we are. We need an image. A name. What do you think about the People's Army?"

"We don't have an army, Pete."

"So, it's symbolic, Bill. And, if we make an impact, perhaps an army sympathetic to our cause will grow."

"I like it, Pete," said Joe.

Mr. X nodded but remained silent.

Feeling he had control of the guys, Peter moved on. "So, Mr. X is a friend I met in Eugene. He's one of those guys that implode buildings when you want them razed. He has the skills we need.

"Let's blow up something here in Astoria. Demand to be heard. Get the people to back us and throw the politicians in prison for their affront to our society."

"You're right, man!"

"Power to the people."

"The Man uses us as stepping stones to their wealth and shares nothing as if we don't exist," Peter declared.

"You got that right."

"We need to unite the masses to become a flame that will burn down the establishment!" Pete stated in a rising voice. "The establishment is killing off the men and women on our campuses. Sending the men to

186

Nam to be slaughtered for the sake of the spread of American colonial power!" Peter dropped his voice for effect. "Guys, Mr. X is the kindling that will light the flame of the oppressed. I submit to you we blow up the John Jacob Astor Hotel."

Peter stopped for effect. To let it sink in. He pointed to an American flag hanging sideways on the wall with a peace sign spray-painted over it.

"Mr. X can help us do that."

Peter scanned the room seeing a bobbing of heads.

"It's a plan then," he declared.

He glanced at his new friend who stood up. A tall man, he had a strong presence, and tired, weather-worn skin. His mutton-chops blended into a thick, black Fu Manchu. His hair was long and wavy but tied back in a ponytail low on his neck. Something about him did not ring true to Bill.

"As Peter alluded, though I have a degree in engineering, I specialize in explosives technology," Mr. X lied. "Peter and I have been down to the underground of Astoria and scoped out the tunnels the town is built upon. The plan we came up with is to implode the John Jacob Astor Hotel. To raze it to the basement below. There will be little above street level but a pile of bricks."

"Wow," Joe let out.

"You can do that?" Bill mumbled his question.

"We can," Mr. X said, "And we will." His confidence was contagious.

"What's in it for you?" Bill questioned.

"I feel your pain, my man. I'm on your side. My reward will be our success."

Everyone was excited to work out the details. Everyone except Bill. He didn't trust anyone that refused a hit on a doobie.

24

JOE HOLED UP IN THE SQUATTER HOME BASEMENT. He had dropped by to see his mom earlier, something he did not do often. Mrs. Lagerstrom didn't understand what he and his generation were going through and the less time he was home, the better. Today, he went home, and his mom started in immediately. 'Where are you staying? You're not doing that LST stuff, are you? You're twenty-three. What are you going to do with your life?' Joe ignored her and headed straight to his room. The windows were painted black with a peace symbol on each. He picked up some things he needed.

"What?" he asked as he slid by her again. "I'll be at Pete's," he stated for no good reason. His mom dropped her arms to her side and, in frustration, watched him leave the house.

Joe returned to the basement, turned on his black light, and grabbed Iron Butterfly's first album, one of his favorites. He set the second side up on his turntable and carefully rested the needle onto the record surface. He threw himself down on his bed pad and closed his eyes as "In-A-Gadda-Da-Vida" began its seventeen-minute musical journey of psychedelic and heavy metal mix. Joe's bedside tables were base speakers which rattled the basement. Joe claimed he "discovered" the group which was true if only among his friends.

He knew everything about the band. This song was written by Ron Ingle, Butterfly's organist and vocalist while drinking a gallon of Red Mountain wine. Bushy, the group's drummer, wrote down the lyrics for the inebriated Ingle as he played it for him. Bushy misinterpreted Ingle's slurred words and what was meant to be *In the Garden of Eden* became the garbled name that stuck.

Joe's mind floated away into a mist of boredom as Bushy's drum solo reverberated his chest.

Tom walked across the spotty grass of the Victorian's backyard and up to the basement door. He threw his shoulder into it without announcement and entered.

He hadn't been to the guy's squat in a while. The mess was frightening. At the Job Corps, if your bed wasn't made and your room 'ship shape,' you got a talking to. If it happened again, you got a demerit. Here it looked like two decades of crap were mixed in a giant blender and thrown in the basement. *Where to sit? Where to stand? Where was the floor?* Tom wasn't sure.

Peter and Joe sat on what once was a couch and Bill was lying on his disgusting mattress. Tom, depressed, sat on the cooler "chair." Silent and sullen.

Joe looked at Pete. *What's up with Tom?*

"Hey, Tom," Peter said, "We've got good news."

Tom looked at him but said nothing.

"I could use some good news," he finally said.

Bill scratched his curly beard. "What's wrong, guy? Never seen you this down."

After a long pause, Tom said, "Ah, nothing, I guess."

"Only a girl causes this much shit."

Tom looked his way. His face said everything.

"Ahah! Dr. Bill scores again. Diagnosis: correct." Bill took a drag and passed it to Joe.

"Whatever," Joe stated, "it's nothing some time with the guys can't cure."

Tom half-smiled, but his heart still hurt.

"Enough about me, guys," Tom stated, "Haven't seen you for a while. What's happening?"

Bill and Joe turned their heads to Peter.

"We are about to embark on a great adventure that will change the military-industrial complex in America forever. It'll blow your mind." Peter held up his hands as if a director describing the next scene in a movie. "You're in, of course."

Tom went along for the moment not knowing what he was getting into. His old friends smoked too much and when they did, their creativity overtook them. You never knew what they would come up with. His life had moved on while theirs had not. Tom looked around at his friends. Bill's tie-dye shirt and bellbottom pants with an embroidered flower said it all.

"So, here's the plan. We create the 'People's Army.' Nice ring to it, huh? Oh, thanks—" Peter took a drag on the doobie being passed around. "We'll start with something explosive to get The Man's attention. The common man will be with us. They understand the shit that goes on in this country. The Army will grow. We'll be a movement! We'll change the country. Fifty years from now, historians will call us the 'founding fathers' of the New America."

There was a silence in the room. Then, all broke into laughter, except Tom. He shook his head. Peter offered the joint to him, but Tom stood up instead.

"I don't have time for this," he stated as he headed for the door.

"Ah, come on, man. Don't be a downer," Pete called out to him.

Tom never looked back, the door slamming shut behind him.

The black GTO, looking like a panther ready to strike, roared to a stop in front of the basement. Mr. X saw a man walking out. Someone not part of the People's Army.

Mr. X entered the basement and called out to Peter,

"Hey, guy. Who was that?" Mr. X was concerned. He wanted control, and any friend that might threaten the plan was a potential problem.

"A friend. Tom. Why?"

"I need to know who I'm dealing with."

"Don't worry about him. Friends for a long time."

"Does he know about our plans?"

"Yeah. Just told him. Thought he would be excited."

"But he wasn't, huh?"

"Nah. All wrapped up in his new life. Got a new girlfriend who's yanking his chain."

"Been there. I'll be right back."

Tom felt the GTO before it pulled up beside him. The glass pack mufflers made a threatening rumble that filled the air.

"Hey," Mr. X called out, "Wait up."

Tom turned.

"Are you Tom?" snarled the driver. All Tom could see was an evil Fu Manchu.

194

"Who wants to know?"

"I'm helping your clueless friends back in the basement. They're working hard on this People's Army thing."

"They need less weed and more brains."

"Not arguing with you, Tom. But they are still your friends, right?"

"Right. But that doesn't mean I want to go to San Quentin with them. Doesn't mean I want to blow up innocent people either. What are you guys thinking? And why are you helping them? What's in it for you?"

"Their idea, Tom. I'm just helping them."

Mr. X worried about this new guy, Tom. He had come too far to let some rogue spoil his plans.

"You guys," Tom said, "can plan this thing all you want, but I am trying to get my life straight. Job Corps has helped a lot. I've got a job at the jewelry store. I've met someone. Things are getting serious… I think. And I'm not about to mess it all up for a pot-induced plan of self-destruction."

"I get it. Let's take a deep breath for a minute. Tell me about your new job at the jewelry store. I may need some stones."

25

CLASS WAS OUT, and Tom walked back to his room, Merri a half a block in front. This was just one of the new protocols, Merri left class first, no communication between them except in class when absolutely necessary. It was a new cold war and had been going on for a week. Tom hated it.

What the hell did I do? Can't think of a damn thing. He worked it over again and again. *How can we get back to where we were?*

After a week, he still had no idea.

Tom started hanging out with his old friends, Bill, Joe, and Peter. But that didn't work. To Tom, it was like going back to 3rd-grade recess. Their People's Army nonsense went from being just stupid to dangerously stupid. Blowing up the Hotel had jail time written all over it. Big time, jail time.

Tom felt low about his relationship with Merri and talked to Larry about it.

"Have patience Tom, she'll come around. It's only been a week."

Easy for him to say.

Merri's mood ranged from angry to melancholy on an hourly swing. Sammi tried to be helpful but had her own boy issues. How to juggle 3 at a time. two townies and a very cute JC kid.

In the week since the 'Blow Up,' Merri spent time with Penny. More than she had in the last couple of months.

"So, who is this Sally?" Merri questioned. "I see her around and she smiles like I should be glad she's stealing my Tom."

"Just a high school classmate. Not even an old girlfriend," Penny replied. They had been over this, more than once.

Penny comforted Merri and enjoyed the time they spent together. But she knew when Tom and Merri got back together, she would be on her own… again.

She wished she could get rid of that thought, but there it was.

"Listen Merri, you're making too much of this. Try talking to Tom. The cold shoulder only goes so far. We both know you're not breaking up over this."

"I don't know that." Merri sounded angry.

"Yes, you do. You two aren't breaking up. One more week of you pissed one minute and poor miserable Merri the next and I'll go nuts. Talk to him."

Sally wasn't done with Tom. Not even close. With Merri and Tom on the outs, her time was now.

Plenty of guys pursued Sally, but the guy she couldn't stop thinking about was the one that wasn't interested in her.

Maybe I like being the one doing the chasing?

She didn't dwell on her motives. She just knew she was far from being done.

December 1

As things went into week 2, Larry called Merri and Tom into his office.

"The Clatsop County Historical Society has asked the Job Corps to help restore the Flavel House foyer. A two-member team each from painting, masonry, and carpentry. You two have been chosen from carpentry. Your instructor will fill you in during class. Congratulations."

And to think I accuse my wife of being a matchmaker! Larry chuckled to himself.

The Flavel House job lasted four days. On the first day, they called an unspoken chilly truce. By the second day, both Tom and Merri realized that being snotty and snide took too much work. Easier to be friendly. Job Corps masonry and painting students did most of the work. That left time for Tom and Merri to talk and explore the historic Victorian mansion.

By the fourth day, Tom and Merri were back together. Tom's parents, doing a bit of matchmaking on their own, invited the kids to a pizza dinner at Shakey's.

And that seemed to seal it. Tom and Merri, an item again.

Salvatore Ferragamo was a good roommate for Tom. An Italian-American from an old-school family, Sal was in the Culinary Arts program at the Job Corps. One time, Tom took him to Shakey's Pizza Parlor for a taste of 'Astoria Italian.'

"Tom, if anyone tried serving this food in my 'hood in Pittsburgh, they'd mercy shoot 'em."

Sal had counseled Tom through the whole Tom/Merri blow up. He did it in an Italian way.

"Sure, you scream, and she yells and then you make up and it's over. It's all about Makeup Sex. Don't ever forget that Tom."

Sal got leave to attend his sister's wedding back in Pittsburgh. And Tom looked forward to some 'Sal free' time. There were some not so good things about Sal as a roommate. Loud, opinionated, and messy, Sal loved clothes, and had more than any guy Tom had known. And more shampoo, cleanser, and moisturizer than any girl. All of it strewn around the room.

With Sal gone, Tom could straighten the place up. The 'new' Tom was a bit of a clean freak.

Sally also knew Salvatore. She teased him about the similarity of their names. Sal knew her intention was to get to Tom, not him. But he didn't mind. Tall, dark, and handsome, Sal wasn't lacking in female attention. If he happened to be Sally's second choice, that was OK with him.

Sal knew something Sally did not. She didn't have a chance with Tom.

They bumped into one another after lunch one day and he told her about his trip back home.

"See you when you get back, Sal."

She imagined Tom without a roommate for five days.

Since their fight, Merri made a few changes in her behavior. She allowed Tom more time without her. They didn't have to be together every moment. She wanted to give him some space, even though he hadn't asked for it.

"A bunch of us are talking about going to the Paul Revere & the Raiders gig at the Armory."

"When?" Merri asked. She wasn't a Paul Revere fan.

"Saturday night. Won't be able to stay for the whole show, cause of curfew. But we can catch the bus back at 10 and see most of it. Should be fun. Want to go?"

"Why don't you go with the group. I should spend a little time with Penny."

"You sure?" Tom was surprised but didn't want to push it.

"You go. Have a good time."

December 6

Saturday came, and Tom and Merri had lunch together at the cafeteria. Then Tom left for basketball with the guys. Merri and Penny planned dinner and a movie at the JC.

The Paul Revere concert was loud, fun, and packed. The crowd jammed the front of the stage. In the mezzanine that circled the floor, some people were making out and others drinking the booze they snuck in.

Tom knew a bunch of people from his high school days. He also saw Bill and Pete, along with the weird guy with the Fu Manchu. That guy gave Tom the creeps.

Tom made it back to the JC in plenty of time to beat curfew. He was sorry Merri hadn't gone, but all in all, a fun evening.

When Tom went into his dorm room, Sally was waiting around the corner of the building. Listening outside, she heard the shower start. She tried the door. It was unlocked. For some reason, guys at JC didn't lock their doors. Which was OK with Sally.

When she got in the room, Sally started taking off her clothes and slid into one of the beds. The perfect picture for when Tom came out of the shower.

Merri thought of Tom all through dinner and the movie. She had never wanted to go to Tom's room in the past. With Sal in Pittsburgh, now seemed to be the right time for a surprise for Tom and a pleasant evening for both.

Slipping through the dark campus, *I'm glad it's not raining,* Merri got to Tom's door. She started to knock, tried the knob, it was unlocked. She went for the surprise and opened the door.

Tom came out of the shower, grabbed a towel, and wandered into the main room, idly drying his hair. Sally lay naked in his bed. Merri came through the door.

And that was it. Merri was done. No amount of explanation from Tom would cover this.

Tom wanted to kill Sally and talk to Merri. But she was gone, and he knew she wasn't coming back. Sally got out of bed and started to get dressed. Tom had dropped the towel when Merri ran. The commotion caused a couple guys from the neighboring rooms to look through Tom's open door.

And then it was all over campus.

Larry was the counselor for all three students involved. His boss had a few things to discuss with Larry.

"Larry, you might not know this, but the federal government did not set up the Job Corps as a pornographic dating service for horny young people."

"Yes, sir."

Sally received a 30-day penalty for curfew violation, another 30 days for being in an opposite-sex dorm room and another for 'conduct unbecoming.' She was grounded on the JC campus for 3 months.

Merri's penalty, 30 days for curfew violation.

Tom, who didn't have anything to do with any of this, got a 15-day penalty for being in the wrong place at the wrong time.

Every time he heard a Paul Revere song on the radio, Tom turned it off.

PART SIX

Reckoning

26

December 1

MERRI STEPPED INTO THE BUS at the guard's gate of Job Corps. The 5:10 bus arrived on time for once. The Job Corps allowed its students personal time on the weekend. There were rules. The JC needed to keep control, but if you proved yourself, if you returned on time, did not drink, or do drugs, you showed the JC strong character. In her present state of mind, Merri cared little about all that.

Merri watched out of the bus window as the world passed by. The same world that came crashing down on her again. Men had failed her... again. She opened up to Tom. He let her down. She needed to forget about it. Re-evaluate what she was doing. Maybe this whole Job Corps thing wasn't for her.

As the bus pulled over at Eighth and Bond, she stepped down and turned up her collar to the blustery offshore wind. She wandered, no destination in mind.

What's wrong with men? Or is it me? I can't have faith in them. They are all liars. They fail me every time. I'm sick of their promises.

She walked by the Golden Star Chinese restaurant as a couple exited the bar door in the back. Laughter filled the air. She decided she needed that now.

The place was busy. Only bar seats available. Merri sat down and studied the people through the mirror that lined the back bar. A local's bar. Relaxed. Casual. Not a lot of sake served at the Golden Star. Mostly a beer drinking crowd. Or whiskey shots.

"Hi. What can I get for you?" Barb was a career bartender. Twenty years at the Golden Star. She knew everyone that came in more than once.

Merri ordered a burger & a coke.

"Honey. It's a Chinese restaurant. A burger, really?"

"I don't know a thing about Chinese. Surprise me."

Four boys sat on bar stools near Merri. Not really boys, she realized, all at least her age. She heard laughter, chatter, and attempts at humor. The oldest of them, the quietest one, turned to Merri.

"I'm Scott." There was one empty stool between him and Merri.

"Merri," She smiled.

"Where you from?' Scott asked to keep the conversation going.

"Portland," Merri lied, finding it easier than explaining the Job Corps.

Barb brought Merri her coke and she and Scott chatted in that kind of fun, kind of awkward way of first meetings.

Then Barb brought the meal. She served Merri pork fried rice, fried shrimp, chicken subgum chow mein or as they called it at the Golden Star, Dinner #4.

"Thanks. But this is a lot of food." The delightful smell overwhelmed Merri. She realized how hungry she was.

"It is a lot of food and all of it good. You look like you could use a filling meal and a little cheering up," was Barb's quick reply. "Hon, do you want chopsticks?"

"I'm not sure..."

"I'll bring both chopsticks and a fork. Tastes better if you use the chopsticks. The effort makes it better." Barb left Merri with her new utensils and enough food to feed a small army.

Mary fumbled with chopsticks. *How on earth do the Chinese get through a meal?* None of the food got to Merri's mouth.

"Can I help you with those?" Scott moved to the stool next to Merri and took the chopsticks out of her hands.

Scott showed her how to use the chopsticks and gave them back to Merri. She fumbled and then got a little better. She tried the fried rice first, no luck.

"The rice is too tiny, try something bigger. Go for the shrimp."

She did, and the first shrimp landed in her lap. The next one made it to her mouth. Then she got cocky and went for the chow mein. In the lap again.

"Scott, can I offer you some of this great food? There is way too much for just me."

Barb brought Scott chopsticks and a fork.

"I didn't realize you two were sharing." She had seen this a thousand times over the years.

"Hey, Merri thank you for your generous offer," Scott said as he dug in using his fork.

"Hey, wait a minute. A fork? Really? No chopsticks, come on!"

"Chopsticks are great if you want to lose 50 pounds fast. If you want to get fed, a fork is the only way. Everybody knows that."

"Everybody but me and the Chinese." Merri put the chopsticks in her purse as a memento and picked up the fork.

The conversation went on and Merri and Scott—truly a man now that Merri had learned he was 24— got to know one another.

"You should have white wine with this dinner. Can I get you a glass? I'm having another beer."

"I don't know. I'm—"

"Come on, Merri, It's Friday Night. Let loose a little."

Merri agreed. Letting loose was exactly what she needed. She was not about to open up to Scott, but it felt good to escape her troubles. She liked the wine too. It had been a while. Suddenly, she remembered the curfew at the Job Corps. Merri checked her watch. The last bus left soon. She had to go.

"Thank you, Scott, for the glass of wine." It was still half full. "Sorry. I have to go." She gave him a frustrated look.

He asked for her phone number. Merri said she was traveling a lot and would be hard to reach. But said she would be back in Astoria soon. Scott gave her his number and she promised she would call.

Merri made the bus in plenty of time. She spent the ride thinking about her nice evening and her new friend. The bus let her off at the Job Corps gate.

As she waited in line with the other JC kids returning from town, Merri flashed on the zero tolerance for drugs and alcohol and the random testing. She would play it cool. What could half a glass of wine do?

When she reached the guard, Merri was chosen for testing.

Job Corps tested in a small building by the front gate. Merri blew a .05 on the Breathalyzer. Barely a bump on the dial. But enough.

The woman doing the testing called the front gate. The front gate informed the Security office and the Head Administrator, and Merri was escorted to her room. The head of Security and the Administrator were waiting for her.

"Merri, as you know the Job Corps has a zero policy for alcohol and drugs. You were told this when admitted. You signed the application agreeing to abide by this policy. You have chosen not to follow it.

"Remove all of your belongings and put them in these two boxes. You will spend the night in Zone 5. We will have a termination meeting tomorrow at 9 AM."

It was a long night.

Described as the 'disciplinary area' of the Job Corps, Zone 5 served as the Brig when Tongue Point was a Navy base. Merri spent the night on a thin mattress in a cell. No lock on the door but the sound of the cell door closing horrified her.

Merri hoped to cry herself to sleep, but sleep didn't come.

December 2

The 'termination meeting' began in the administrator's office. Present were the Security Chief, the Admissions officer, Merri's counselor Larry, two Student Representatives, the Administrator, and Merri. The room was small and windowless; everyone except the Administrator stood. Defenseless, Merri felt alone in the crowded room.

As painful as the meeting was, it was brief.

"Merri, you have broken the rules of the Job Corps. Your stay at Tongue Point has been terminated. In this envelope is a one-way ticket to Portland. Also enclosed is a voucher for three days at Grace Gospel Mission off Burnside in Portland. After that, you are on your own."

The Administrator slipped the envelope across the desk. Merri, shattered, only stared at it. Everyone was crying.

One of the best students the Job Corps had produced was getting kicked out.

The Administrator finally broke the silence. "This second envelope I'm handing you contains a one-way ticket from Portland back to Astoria. After your stay at the Mission, if you decide to come back and adhere to every rule, use the ticket to get back to the Job Corps. If you decide not to come back, turn the ticket in at the Greyhound depot. It's worth $18."

"Also enclosed is $50. The ticket and the money are being given to you by the people in this room, in the hope that you will come back and finish the success you started."

Merri was driven to the Greyhound bus depot on the side of the John Jacob Astor Hotel in downtown Astoria.

December 2

Merri didn't know what to do. Couldn't think, couldn't concentrate. Exhausted, her mind kept going, whirling in a circle. Faster and faster.

In a moment of clarity, it came to her, she should call Miss Silver. Someone she trusted, someone who understood. Miss Silver would know what to do.

Merri crossed the lobby to a bank of four built-in phone booths of dark stained wood that framed etched glass inserts. She grasped a sculpted brass handle and opened a booth. As she entered, a domed, overhead light came on. She stood, her finger shaking as she dialed "0."

"I need to make a long distance collect call to Redmond, Oregon to the Redmond Grade School. Person to person with Miss Eunice Silver, from Merri Sue Morrison." Merri said all this in a high, wavering voice she did not recognize as her own.

"Thank you, placing the call now."

Merri felt better already. Except the person at the grade school office wouldn't take the call.

Merri tried again.

"We don't take collect calls here."

Merri tried again, crying now.

"Tell her its Merri Sue, I have to talk to her." Merri screaming now, her voice heard all through the lobby. People were looking.

At the Redmond Grade School, the aide in the office told the principal, Mr. Sanderson, about the repeated calls. He walked down to Miss Silver's classroom.

"If she calls again please, come get me. I'll reimburse the school for the call."

"No need for that Miss Silver. I'll send Jennifer down if there is another call. She can watch your class for you."

Merri left the phone booth and went to the lobby restroom. Washed her face, calmed down. Then waited five minutes and called again.

"Redmond Grade School, Jennifer speaking. Yes, we will accept the call, please hold the line and I will get Miss Silver for you."

The sound of Miss Silver's voice sent a wave of relief flowing through Merri Sue. And she told her everything. All about Tom, how wonderful everything had been and then how he had betrayed her. And then Scott, nice and friendly, forced her into drinking. Her counselor, Larry, was supposed to help her. He had helped her alright, right out of the Job Corps.

"Give me your number Merri. I need to think about this and call you back in 5 minutes."

It didn't take her five minutes.

"Merri, it is Miss Silver and I want you to listen to me carefully. You were given a wonderful opportunity. The help you needed was put in front of you. And what have you done with it? You have placed blame for your misfortune on everyone but yourself."

"But I—"

"I have helped you all I can, Merri. Now the help must come from you. From within you."

"But I tried and then Tom—"

"Merri, haven't you heard what I've said. Look within for your answers and—"

Calvin Cahail & Jim Hallaux

But Merri couldn't take anymore. It felt like her world would split. She softly rested the receiver in its cradle.

27

December 2

IN THE EVENING, Sammi came back to the dorm room she shared with Merri Sue. Except Merri was not there and her belongings... gone. She ran over to Penny's room. Merri not there either. Penny had not seen her since the morning classes.

Penny and Sammi went over to the student lounge. There were still kids hanging around. No one had seen or heard from Merri Sue.

The two women spent another hour scouring the Job Corps campus looking for Merri. Their last stop was the security gate. The attendant not all that helpful.

"I will note you reported Merri not in her room at curfew and will notify the Security Chief in the morning. Thank you for bringing this to our attention."

December 3

A notice appeared on each student's door:

> *This is to inform you that*
> *Merri Sue Morrison has been terminated*
> *from Job Corp for policy infraction.*

At breakfast, there were a million different rumors concerning Merri bouncing around the cafeteria. Arrested, kidnapped, caught in the men's locker room, drinking & drugs, and on and on. With each retelling, the rumors became more lurid.

Tom was the last person to hear about Merri's disappearance. After the 20th wild story, he headed to the one person that should know. Larry Alred.

Tom arrived at Larry's office, out of breath and more than a little out of his mind.

"Larry, you got to tell me what's going on with Merri. Where is she? What happened?"

"I can't give you any specifics, Tom. Job Corps policy doesn't allow me to divulge personal student information to other students. This is a personal matter."

"Cut the shit, Larry. Just tell me what happened."

"First off watch your mouth. And remember who you are talking to. For the rest of this conversation, which will be brief, you will address me as Mr. Allred."

"OK... OK... I'm sorry. I'm worried, really worried."

"Understandably so. Sit down, collect your thoughts and we can talk."

Larry busied himself with some papers on his desk. Tom sat stewing and fidgeting, but finally calmed down.

Larry seemed to sense the calm and gave what little information he could.

"The Job Corps has very stringent rules and Merri broke one. The outcome is that she was removed from campus."

"Where is she now? No one's seen her?" Tom struggled to keep his voice even.

"I can't tell you that, I'm sorry Tom."

"How do I get in touch with her?"

"I don't know. If she chooses to, she knows how to get in touch with you."

"I could call her parents. She probably went home. You have an address and phone number. Right?"

"That's information I can't share with you, Tom. I must go by the book on this. I've told you more than I should have."

And in that instant, Tom realized how little he knew about the most important person in his life.

'I have counseling sessions beginning right now and then staff meetings after that. Stop by after 5 tonight and we can come up with a plan on how you can deal with this." Larry's new concern was Tom.

But Tom didn't stop by that afternoon. He retreated to his room and stayed there for two days. Didn't leave. Tom asked his roommate to tell everyone he was sick.

And he was. Tom's body shut down, but his mind would not stop spinning.

What rule did she break?

Where is she? Who is she with?

My fault? Merri was one in a million.

I lost her.

28

December 1

ANDRE AND PETE HAD MOVED on from the Portway, down Marine Drive, and across the street to the Worker's Tavern. So far this week it was their 5th night of non-stop drinking.

"I need you to do me a favor." Andre snarled at Pete.

"Sure, what do you need?" Pete's reply was quick.

"I need you to shut up and do something." Andre's eyes were bloodshot and his voice was harsh. "For the last two weeks, all you have done is talk… and talk and talk. Now you need to do something."

"Do what?"

"What'd you mean what? You're the one talking about making a statement. Showing the Man."

"Yeah show —"

"Enough talking. You want to blow up this Astor Hotel. Well… stop talking and do it."

Andre had put Pete in his place and Pete knew it.

"But we don't have the explosives." Pete started to sweat.

"You get the C-4, I'll pay for it, and we'll blow the damn thing up." Andre showed every sign of being done with Pete.

"I have a bunch of questions about how—" Pete's voice sounded high and weak.

"The only question that matters is, are you and your boys in or not? You have until I finish this drink to decide." Andre threw his MacNaugton shot back and slammed the glass down on the bruised bar top.

29

December 3

THE BLUE AND SILVER GREYHOUND BUS turned the corner into the station in downtown Portland. The last time Merri was here was the day she left for Astoria and the Job Corps.

Now she was back. Defeated.

She looked at the address and decided to walk the three blocks to Grace Gospel Mission. She turned off Burnside. The narrow side street was lined with three-story buildings, weathered, and stained with age. Sculpted dual-lamp street lights stood like soldiers up and down the road.

Merri stared at the shelter in front of her, shabby suitcase in hand. A fire escape ladder hung from the

227

side of the nondescript building. Blackwater stains painted the siding beneath the small, wood-framed windows. The white-painted wood siding needed attention. A sign, rocking with a rusty, rhythmic squeal, hung above a door; Grace Gospel Mission. Merri glanced at the information Job Corps had given her.

Is this the right place?

The dark wood door resisted opening as Merri tugged hard on it. Inside, a room 150 feet long held row after row of bed pads laid on the floor, each with a single wool blanket folded on top. The high ceiling had a row of windows that let in weak light casting a dank aura over the room. A woman in her forties in a dark dress with a full, white apron, mopped the floor. She stopped, leaned on the mop's handle, and stared at Merri. The woman raised her arm and pointed to a room in the back with a large window. Inside the room, another woman busied herself shuffling papers. Merri walked through the open door. The woman looked up, smiled, and welcomed Merri.

"Good afternoon. Come in. Sit, please." The woman pointed to an old, second-hand desk chair with sculpted arms in front of her desk. Merri sat and handed the woman the paper Job Corps had given her. "My name is Nerissa." She looked at the paper. "Merri. Welcome to Grace Gospel Mission."

Merri nodded but said nothing. Nerissa had dealt with all kinds. She was patient.

"Well, this will be your home for the next three days. You understand you need to arrange to stay somewhere else after that?"

Merri nodded.

Nerissa noticed Merri was clean and moderately dressed. Above average physically for Grace Gospel Mission. But emotionally? That was another matter.

"Next to us are the restroom facilities and showers." Nerissa reached behind herself into a cardboard box sitting on the dull carpet. She grabbed a small paper bag and handed it to Merri. "You'll find soap, toothpaste, brush, and a few other kindnesses donated by our supporters. Keep these with you. You are responsible for all your things."

Nerissa watched Merri barely glance into the bag.

"Pastor John is here weekdays every afternoon from two until four. If you need someone to talk to, he is a great man. Portland is a big city. Let me know if I can help you get around. We offer coffee and donuts or eggs depending on donations between six and eight in the morning. Soup supper is at six. Lights out at ten. Any questions?"

Merri shook her head. Nerissa gave her a second, then said,

"All right then. Let me know if I can help. Good luck, Merri."

Nerissa stood with a smile on her face. Merri nodded her head goodbye and left the office. The woman mopping the floor stopped and watched the lost girl with her suitcase.

"It will be time for supper in less than an hour. People will start coming in. Claiming beds. I suggest you pick one and lay claim to it. This one here is still in good shape."

Merri nodded and walked over to it. She knelt and glanced around the room.

How had it come to this?

She heard clanking of pots and pans on the far side of the room. Volunteers were setting up supper. Merri laid down on her pad in the fetal position and fell asleep.

Merri fought to wake up. She felt someone pushing on her shoulder. Merri looked up as a man with a full, tangled burnt-orange beard, stared down at her.

"This is my bed," he stated. She smelled whiskey on his breath. His weathered face with its deep crow's feet told of a man that had spent his life under the sun. "This is MY bed," he restated. His straw-woven cowboy hat, bent with character, showed years of dirt as did his over and under-sized clothing. He began to rant. "This is my bed," he declared. No one around paid him any attention. Except for the lady that earlier was mopping the floor.

"Now, Joseph. There are many good beds in the men's section. She's a nice girl, right? It's her first night. Be kind. Help me out. How about this one over here?"

"Okay," he said, and the woman led him over to the other bed. As she returned, she winked at Merri who just sat there as if comatose.

After a few minutes, Merri laid back down and slept through supper.

December 4

Merri woke with a start. The room was dark, and the beds were full. An off odor permeated the room. One woman called out loud to her deceased sister. When was she coming to visit, she asked? They needed to plan the wedding. Several others snored through it all. Merri stared out the high windows. The streetlights veiled the stars. Like Merri's future, they could not be seen. Exhausted, Merri found sleep again as the woman continued talk of a wedding that would be.

The smell of coffee filled the room. Many sat on their beds eating stale donuts and drinking thin coffee. Half the overnighters had already left. Merri walked over to the breakfast table. Nothing looked appealing, but she was famished. She took a donut and the cup of coffee handed to her and went back to her bed. The donut gone in seconds.

The mop lady, Ruth was her name, had returned to work and watched Merri. Ruth brought another donut to Merri and knelt next to her. Merri smiled as she received the pastry. Ruth patted Merri on the shoulder as she rose to return to her duties.

As Merri slowly finished her coffee, the room cleared out, the volunteers cleaned up the food line, and Ruth set about pulling the blankets on the hundred-plus beds. As she worked her way up a row, she neared Merri. She sat next to her again.

"You need to figure out what to do," Ruth said. "Don't you have a friend or relative where you can stay a while?"

Merri knew Ruth was right. The family she nannied for might help. They were close by. Merri looked at Ruth but said nothing. She reached for her suitcase.

"The bus stop," Ruth offered, "is two blocks down and a right turn."

Merri nodded and left.

She headed for the stop. As she walked, she tried to comb her hair with her hands. She should have showered while at Grace Gospel Mission, but it felt dirty to her. Now she felt dirty. She found the bus stop and stood there as several buses passed by. She was ashamed to plead with the Clintons to give her shelter.

Merri was lost.

In the end, she turned and wandered aimlessly through the streets of Portland.

At three, she returned to the shelter. Pastor John sat at a small wooden table near Nerissa's office. Merri chose a different pad. She wanted nothing to do with Joseph, the crazy man from last night. She stowed her suitcase by the bed pad and sat watching the pastor. He looked up and smiled. Merri looked down. Alone, she sat on the bed. An hour later, as the pastor was leaving, he walked by Merri.

"Hi," he said, "I'm Pastor John." He waited for a response but did not receive one. "Have a blessed day." With that, the pastor left.

Right before six, Joseph returned to the shelter and saw Merri on 'his' bed. He walked over.

"That's my bed," He declared.

Merri did not want a problem and moved. Grabbing her suitcase, she would sleep somewhere else. Merri Sue chose a bed two over and set her case down.

"That's my bed," Joseph stated behind Merri in a loud voice. She turned. Merri realized no matter which bed she chose; the crazy old man would declare it his.

Just then, Ruth came over.

"Cowboy Joe, come on. Leave the pretty girl alone. Wasn't it nice that she gave you your bed over here?" She walked Joseph back to the first bed.

Another woman a bed over spoke up.

"Ruth, he is here all the time. What happened to the three-night rule?"

"The owner's son," she whispered. Merri looked at Joseph with new understanding.

December 5

On Merri's third day at Grace Gospel Mission, she had yet to use the showers. Yet to speak to the pastor. Yet to ask Nerissa for help. She roamed the streets. Lost. Before soup supper, Nerissa asked Merri to join her in her office.

"Merri, this is your last night here. You realize that, right?"

Merri nodded.

"Pastor John tells me you have not spoken to him. You have not asked me for anything either. What are you going to do tomorrow?"

Merri shrugged her shoulders. Nerissa knew Merri did not belong in this environment. She reached into her desk and pulled out a business card.

"Here is a card for The Sisters of Mary. Go there. Promise me you will at least do that."

Merri looked at the card.

"It's close by. They won't badger you about religious stuff."

Merri nodded.

"Good. You come to see me any time. Just to say hi. Or if you need help."

Merri stood up. It was time for soup.

30

December 5

A BITING DECEMBER BREEZE found a crack in Merri's coat. She pulled its collar tighter around her neck. The sky cast a gray hue over the town and her mood. She looked back at Grace Gospel Mission. It had depressed her when she first arrived there. Now she was walking away. She turned to face the city around her.

She could not get warm. Her bones shook. She passed a building whose front was all glass. Inside, a young man in coveralls with 'Jack' embroidered on them polished the latest new cars. She looked up. 'Chevrolet,' said the sign.

The man smiled at her. She knew nothing about cars, but it would be warmer inside. She pulled on the glass door and entered. He stood up to greet her.

"Good morning," he said.

Merri nodded.

"We're not open yet."

Merri slid her hand over the fender of a baby blue and white Bel Air. Jack checked her out. Her clothes were unkept. Her hair a mess. His boss would be upset if he let a homeless person in the showroom. It was bad for business.

Merri's stomach growled. Her body warmed up. The shaking stopped. She giggled and danced through the Biscaynes and Corvairs. Her arms flailed. The man believed her to be crazy. Was she?

"Look. You'll have to leave. My boss will be here any minute."

Merri ignored him, continuing to dance.

"Seriously," he said grabbing her arm. She stopped dancing glaring at him in fear. Merri ran from the showroom floor returning to her Nowhere World.

She walked, head down. *Men. Always cause problems for me.*

"New to all this, huh?"

Merri was caught off guard. She looked up. There, bundled on a park bench, sat Cowboy Joe. He never looked up, his eyes hidden under the brim of his straw hat. She kept walking.

"You'll find temporary warmth at the library. Down Burnside to 3rd. Left three blocks."

He knew where her head was at. He had seen it countless times in the past.

Merri kept walking. The last thing she needed was another man, crazier than most, telling her what to do. As she walked, the wind pelting her face, his idea sounded better and better. She turned on 3rd and headed north. As she entered through the library's double doors, the warmth swept over her.

She stayed there all day except for the purchase of two hot dogs from a street vendor a block away. Merri flipped through Life and Time and Sunset magazines unable to focus on any of it. An article on building a new home caught her eye and made her think about her carpentry training at Job Corps. About Tom. Her heart saddened.

"We'll be closing in five minutes," a librarian announced to Merri.

Merri nodded. Donned her coat and grabbed the suitcase. Walking down 3rd, she glanced up the side street bordering the library. A homeless man had wrapped himself in a worn sleeping bag under the library's boiler vent. Merri neared the man. He looked up at her. She outstretched her arm asking if she could join him. He gave her an 'I don't care what you do' look and closed his eyes.

Merri pulled the last copy of the Oregonian from a nearby newspaper stand and lay on the hard cement sidewalk. With the paper draped over her, she struggled to insulate herself from the night's cold bite. Despite the harsh environment, exhaustion overcame her, and she fell asleep.

December 6

The body ached. The joints stiff. Merri stretched reaching to the sky. She was famished and decided to treat herself to a good breakfast. She found a cheap diner, sat at the counter, and ordered two eggs with bacon, hash browns, and a glass of orange juice. The guy sitting next to her got up, so she quickly grabbed the newspaper he left behind.

It bored her. All they talked about was the Viet Nam war. She tired of it. Many of her school friends had died over there or disappeared to Canada to avoid the draft. One friend, Tony, 'disappeared' and every year at Christmas time, government agents visited Tony's mom asking her if she had heard from him. Everyone, they said, connects at Christmas. She would tell them no. They would press her for the truth, and she would break down in tears. Sad.

She pushed the paper away and finished her eggs. As she accepted the third refill of coffee, she decided she needed a game plan. Late that afternoon, she would go to the couple she nannied for, humble herself, and seek help. *Could I nanny for them again?*

The paper said it would reach 62 degrees today. She headed for the park close to Grace Gospel Mission. She would spend time people watching until the Clinton's got home.

As she entered the park, she saw Cowboy Joe on a bench with a shopping cart full of his possessions next to him. A tarp was tied down over them. She changed her path. He noticed.

"I can help you," he called out.

Right. Like you've helped yourself.

She continued to walk.

Cowboy Joe let her be.

31

T HE BUS HEAVED LEFT THEN RIGHT as it headed from Job Corps down Leif Erickson Boulevard to downtown Astoria. Tom winced as the driver threw the stick shift into third, grinding its gears. Rain pelted the windshield. His mind never stopped thinking of Merri.

Where is she?

It was Saturday night and no Merri to share it with.

Where is she?

As Tom got off the bus at the terminal next to the John Jacob Astor Hotel, wind gusts drove the rain sideways smacking his face. He tightened his jacket collar. He lingered in the station for the rainfall to ease but lost patience. It was only twelve blocks to the guy's basement. No problem.

The winter sun had set long ago, and the temperature had dipped into the forties. He looked forward to the basement not because it offered warmth but at least it was dry.

Tom shoved the door open. The usual suspects, Pete, Joe, and Bill were hanging out. The new guy, Mr. X, sat next to Pete.

"Hey, Tom," someone called out. "Come on in. We're just laying plans to put the People's Army on the map."

Tom nodded and, kicking debris aside, created a space to sit on the floor.

Peter took charge.

"Tom, Mr. X was just saying we need two blocks of C-4. I have a connection in southern California. Bill and Joe are going with me to get it. Any chance you can come with us?"

"Not for the next couple of months."

"Too bad, my friend. It's our big plan. First step: make a statement. We demolish the John Jacob Astor Hotel."

"Because?"

"Because we can! We're the People's Army. The 'Man' will learn he must reckon with us. We get attention from the masses. They rally behind us. We demand the 'Man' deal with us."

Peter bobbed his head waiting for Tom's endorsement. Mr. X looked on, analyzing each young man's face, their reactions. Bill was exploring his ear wax. Joe retied his Keds' shoelaces. Mr. X had worked with many idiots in the past. He wanted to understand how these idiots would react. How they might wreck HIS plan.

Tom was incredulous. While the government was in a full-scale war dropping napalm on Charlie in Nam, his friends thought they could take on the United States with a couple blocks of C-4.

"Seriously? What happened to the guys I used to hang with? Not a care in the world. Now you want to blow up the world."

"With Mr. X's expertise in explosives, yes," Peter said.

"So, Mr. X is the expert, but you guys need to supply the C-4?"

"And?"

"And why doesn't Mr. X have the connections if he's dealt with explosives?"

"Well, his connection died in an accidental explosion," Pete stated.

"This is sounding better by the minute."

Tom looked at this Mr. X guy who only stared back at him. Peter tried to regain control.

"You're not seeing the big picture, Tom."

"I can see enough. You guys are knuckleheads."

"Hear out our plan," Peter begged. "You'll see it makes sense."

Tom calmed down. He came to see the guys to get his mind off Merri. This should be entertaining. Stupid, but entertaining.

If Pete could somehow find his Southern Cal explosives source, the guys would head down to pick it up.

The chances of any of this happening were about zero.

The winter solstice was the Sunday, December 21st, at 5:21 pm. They will blow the hotel then, declare it a new season for America, and their movement will begin.

The solstice is not a season, Tom thought, *just the shortest day of the year. These guys should have stayed in college!*

"Well, I've heard enough. Much as I share your hopes for a better country, I can't be part of this. My life is in a good place right now." *Assuming I find Merri.* "Good luck."

Tom stood.

"Whoa. Don't go. We've got some good shit to smoke. Stay and enjoy."

"Sorry, guys. I've gotta catch the bus back."

Andre watched him leave.

"Can we trust him? He's not going to rat on us, is he?"

Joe shook his head as he watched Tom leave. *He's going to miss out on all the fun.*

Andre stepped out of the basement.

"Hey, Tom."

Tom turned to see what Mr. X wanted.

"I confess I am a bit nervous about working with the People's Army guys," Mr. X pretended to confide in Tom. "Easy for them to make a mistake. Say the wrong thing. Get scared and rat on their friends… or me. I don't know."

"Not the sharpest knives in the drawer, for sure, but loyal, yes," Tom told him.

"Still, if something were to go wrong, it's a lot of years in the pen. I need a backup plan. Some insurance. You hear me?"

"I'm not sure."

"I mean, while the hotel blows up, the chaos that will follow would be a great cover for something else. Something rewarding to us. Just you and me."

"Like?"

"You asked, 'What's in it for me,' right? Well, across the street from the hotel is a bank. If the hotel blows, why couldn't the bank go too?"

"Are you out of your mind? That's a Federal crime."

"Yeah. You're right. Well, it was a thought. Some extra money would get you and this girl you like off to a good start, huh?"

"Yeah. But I'm not blowing a bank. Period."

"Okay. Okay." Andre pretended to think some more. "Wait. What about this jewelry store you're working at? No Feds involved."

"Stop. I told you, I'm trying to clean up my life… not destroy it."

"Right. Well, think about it at least. Let me know if you change your mind."

32

December 7

"SO, LET ME GET THIS STRAIGHT," the officer said, "a group of guys wants to blow up a hotel to make a name for themselves and take over the world. That about sum it up?"

"Well," Tom said. He felt stupid but had to report what his friends were planning. "I didn't say they were intelligent. But they're serious, sir."

"Look. This is the FBI. We take all threats seriously. But it challenges credibility. Why a small hotel in a small town in nowhere, Oregon?"

"It's Astoria. The first town established west of the Rockies."

"Spare me the 'Rah-Rah."

"Sorry."

"Look. I've got the guys' information and yours. I'll put someone on it. Don't worry. We're the good guys."

"But we don't have a lot of time, sir."

"Are you suggesting we are inefficient, son?"

"Well, no, but I—"

"Let us do our job, okay? Thank you for being a good citizen."

"You're welcome," Tom said. He hung up the black phone handle on its base and looked at the receptionist at Job Corps. "Thank you for your help."

"You have called the Police, the Sheriff, and the FBI. You've done all you can."

She smiled, and Tom left.

33

December 8

SECURING THE EXPLOSIVES hadn't been all that hard. There were certain logistical problems but getting two blocks of C-4 only took Pete three days on the phone. He followed a lead from a guy who had been in jail with a guy who had experience with black market explosives. Both guys were back in jail again.

After the fateful meeting with Mr. X in the basement, Pete, Bill, and Joe decided to get the explosives in Southern California and bring them back to Astoria. Mr. X supplied money for the C-4 and provided a used Chevy truck of dubious ownership.

The hard part would be getting the C-4 from San Ysidro, CA to Astoria, OR. And Mr. X wouldn't be doing any of that.

The drive to San Ysidro, one stop away from Mexico, was long, boring & hot, but without incident.

After a brief but pointed discussion, two M112 blocks of C-4 with detonators were laid before them. The olive-colored mylar-wrapped containers held a pressure-sensitive adhesive on its side. Just as Mr. X said.

The actual buy was like every drug deal the guys had been in. A lot of mistrust on both sides; not much civility and no lack of guns.

On the return trip to Astoria, Bill took the lead drive while Joe crashed. Pete stretched out sideways on the bench seat in the back. A stale burnt smell permeated the cabin. Bill pulled to the side of the freeway.

"What's goin' on?" Joe questioned in a groggy voice.

"Not sure," Bill replied. "I'll look."

Bill popped the truck's hood and ducked, steam blowing out from all sides. As the vapor cleared, Bill

252

saw water spewing from the radiator and from two rubber hoses feeding the engine. He closed the hood which jarred Joe awake again.

Returning to the cab, Bill sat in silence, mulling their options.

Joe slapped him on the arm. "Everything all right?"

"No," Bill replied, "It's not. The truck gave up the ghost. We're sitting ducks here on the freeway with a load of C-4 in the back, and CHP might pull over any second."

Joe scanned the side of the freeway eyeing a strip center a hundred yards away. He leaned his head right, pointing out to Bill the myriad of cars in front of the shops. With a big smile and experience in the matter, Joe opened his door to go get other transport.

"I'll be right back."

Joe headed down the embankment lining the freeway and jumped the chain link fence with a grunt and a groan. Standing in low brush, he took a leak before heading toward the parking lot. He meandered through the vehicles until he found what he was looking for: a set of keys hanging from the ignition. *Was it stealing when an owner leaves his keys like that? It's like an invitation!* Scanning the lot for witnesses, he jumped into the VW van, turned the engine over, and, hearing a satisfying rumble from its engine, put the van in reverse and returned to pick up the guys.

Joe pulled up behind the truck. Bill rolled down his window as he approached.

"Let's go while the getting's good," Joe said.

The desperados grabbed their things and, more importantly, the C-4, and piled into the VW. As they pulled away, all looked at one another but said nothing. They were still in control.

Joe had taken over driving and exited the freeway at its first off-ramp.

"I want to swap these plates," he said. All understood the reasons so did not question him. They found a car in a less visible area and, deed done, were heading North again in a few minutes.

After three hard days of driving, stopping only to pee, for coffee and gas, in that order, they arrived back in Astoria.

34

THE GUY'S IDEA of where the C-4 was to be stored changed many times. It turned out a remote, abandoned cabin wasn't abandoned, just neglected and to make matters worse, owned by a deputy sheriff. Next, an empty warehouse was too near a busy fish station. Finally, through yet another friend of very mixed character, they chose Tongue Point.

Tongue Point is just that. A point of land jutting North out from shore into the Columbia River. It is two miles in length and a half mile wide hemmed in on the western shore side by the US Coast Guard and on the eastern shore by 75 moth-balled Liberty ships from WW ll. In the middle was the sprawling Job Corps campus. The Job Corps was new, but the campus buildings were all repurposed Navy Quonset huts, staff buildings, and even a brig. All from WW II.

The Coast Guard, Job Corps, and Liberty ships took just a small bit of Tongue Point, all near the mainland. The actual point of Tongue Point, stretching almost 1¾ miles, was not used. Heavily forested, fenced off. 'No Trespassing – US Government' signs everywhere. Dark, mysterious, and foreboding.

Bill and Pete had never been on the Point and didn't know of anyone who had. There were rumors of tracer bullets racing out from Tongue Point at fishing boats that had come too close during WW II.

Pete had a friend, whose name was never really known, who claimed to have been on the Point several times and had seen pillboxes, bunkers, and underground passageways. All perfect spots to hide and store explosives.

The fact that all the pillboxes, bunkers, and passageways were old, damp and in some areas downright wet did not appear to have been noticed.

On a moonless night in mid-December, with rain blowing sideways, Bill and Pete paddled hard towards shore in a leaking rubber raft. A fishing boat dropped them off 100 yards from Tongue Point. $100 to the skipper; no questions asked or answered.

The Columbia River at Tongue Point is 6 miles wide. Just off the Point is a 100 feet deep hole. Prized by fisherman, they say it is where the big sturgeon live. The Columbia River off Tongue Point nears the end of its 1,300-mile journey from British Columbia. At low tide, the river screamed by the Point, angry and crazed in its fury to get to the Pacific.

Bill and Pete were interested in the big picture, not the details. They hadn't checked a tide book and found it amazing that what should have taken minutes had taken an hour and a half of desperate paddling. They shot by the east side of the Point, their original destination, and had only beached on the west side when the raft hit a floating snag and the log took them to within 50 feet of shore. Swimming the rest of the way, dragging the raft behind them, they made the rocky beach.

Now in the dark and the cold, they needed to find the pillboxes and bunkers and hide the explosives. That took an hour. It involved crawling along the shoreline; slippery and mean. Then a climb of 150 feet up a very steep hill to the top of Tongue Point. They found the bunker by falling into the below-ground entryway.

Finding the driest place in the bunker, they placed the C-4 on wooden pallets left in the bunker; covered this with a tarp they dragged with them from the raft and topped the whole thing off with branches gathered

257

from above ground. Mission accomplished, the two guys headed backed down the cliff and across the beach to the other side of the Point.

By a miracle, they found the deflated raft and got back on the Columbia heading down river towards Astoria. The tide had changed to slack, so while it didn't help them, at least it didn't work against them.

Exhausted, they pulled out at the old Ferry Landing at 14th Street and walked to their basement squat in Uppertown Astoria. All in all, a wet, cold, miserable night for Bill and Peter.

But one they knew would make them famous for a long time.

35

MERRI SAT ON THE PARK BENCH all morning trying to figure out what to do. She decided to go to the Clintons, the couple she had worked for as a nanny. By the time she made it there, they would be home from their jobs. She reached down for her suitcase, but it was not there. Merri turned, shaken. She looked under the bench. Around the area. Nothing.

She dropped to the bench. Could it get any worse? She carried what money she had left in the pocket of her blouse, but everything else was in the suitcase. She laid her head on the back of the bench and wept. Cowboy Joe just watched.

When she ran out of tears, she regrouped, went to the bus stop, and boarded the bus that would take her to the Clintons' home. They would help her, she knew.

As she gazed out of the bus window, she noted the sky filling with ominous dark clouds. Before her stop, the roof of the bus pinged with raindrops. Two blocks to the Clinton's. She ran. By the time she stood on the porch of their home, her clothes dripped water. Her hair hung wet. Her skin showed streaks of dirty water marks. The streets had taken their toll.

There was no turning back. She rang the doorbell. Merri saw movement behind the half-glass door covered with frilly curtains. The porch light came on. A woman, not Mrs. Clinton, pulled open the curtain.

"May I help you?" the unknown woman asked.

Merri thought for a second.

"Well, I—" she hesitated, "I'm looking for the Clinton's." She checked the address. This was the right house.

"They're not here. Go away now." The woman was uncomfortable with Merri's presence. She looked like a street urchin.

"When will they return?" Merri yelled through the glass.

"They do not live here anymore. Now, go away."

"But they HAVE to live here. I must talk to them. They're my only hope." Merri dropped to the floor of the porch and started to cry.

"Go away, I said. If you don't, I will call the police."
The woman was active in the community and the
homeless situation in the area frustrated her.

"Please, how can I reach them? It is important that I
talk to them."

The woman inside let the drapes fall, walked to the
table phone, and dialed '0.'

"Yes, I need a squad car to come by the house. I have
a vagrant harassing me at my door." She gave her
address and reminded the dispatcher she was a sister-
in-law to the chief. She returned to the door and
opened the curtain. "Hey you, I have called the cops.
I suggest you go home before they get here."

"I have no home," Merri mumbled.

"What?"

"Never mind."

"Go on now."

Merri, still on the porch floor, shuffled over to the
corner next to a potted rose bush long in need of
water. She curled up in a ball.

A black Dodge with white doors and a PPD logo
pulled up to the curb, lights flashing but without
sirens. A fifteen-year vet, Sergeant Hanson, exited
the passenger side door while an eager rookie sitting
behind the wheel reported in. Hanson approached the

door expecting it to open by the man of the house as usual. Instead, the curtain opened, and a pair of large eyes peered out. He looked down at Merri who did not move.

Hanson motioned for the woman to come outside.

"Is it safe?"

"I believe I have the subject under control, ma'am."

"Okay then."

She opened the door staring at Merri, a broom in her hands. She held it as if a weapon.

"You won't be needing that," the officer said.

"Okay."

The rookie joined the Sergeant on the porch.

"Ma'am, what happened here?" Hanson asked.

"Well, this person was looking for the previous owners. I told her they do not live here any longer, but she would not leave."

"And?"

"And, what?"

"What else happened?"

"Well, I demanded she leave but she kept asking about the Clinton's."

"And?"

"And, what?"

"What else happened?"

"Well, that's about it. I don't like her kind around here. This is a nice community. We want to keep it that way."

"So, she didn't threaten you? Hurt you? Break your property? Anything?"

"Well, no, I guess not."

Hanson sighed.

"Should we take her in?" the rookie suggested. He got a hard look from Hanson and backed down.

To the woman that owned the house, Hanson said, "Ma'am, you can go inside now. I'll handle it from here."

She nodded a firm confirmation feeling proud she had done the right thing.

Despite a bad knee, Hanson knelt.

"Hey, what is your name?"

"Merri," she said looking up.

"Mary. My mom's name. How can we help you?"

"I'm lost."

Calvin Cahail & Jim Hallaux

"You mean you need directions?"

"No. I'm lost." She repeated louder as if that helped him understand.

The police officer stared at her wet cheeks.

"You mean you have nowhere to go?"

Merri hesitated, then nodded.

"No family? No friends?"

She shook her head.

"Well, there's a shelter down a way. We could take you there."

"I've been there. They made me leave."

"I see." He thought a moment. "Tim, you were right. We need to run this woman downtown."

The younger officer reached for his cuffs. The elder held up his hand.

"That won't be necessary, Tim."

"Right."

"Help her into the car."

"Yes, sir."

As they walked into the precinct, Hanson winked at the Desk Sergeant. Merri would not be formally processed. Nothing would go on her record. They led

264

her to a cell and left the door ajar. She got free room and board. It was justice. She was obviously not a street person.

Merri enjoyed the bed and food, but it was too soon for her to appreciate the officers' act of kindness.

PART SEVEN

Burnt money

36

December 19

*A*NDRE, *THAT'S WHAT THE ASSHOLE'S NAME IS, why does everyone call him Mr.X?*

Bill sat at the counter of the Coffee Shop at the John Jacob Astor Hotel. Pissed.

Andre treated Pete and Bill like slaves. So bad that Joe stopped going with them – his excuse? His job at the tavern. They entered the tunnels every night for three weeks. Looking for the right place to hide the explosives they needed to implode the JJA Hotel.

Andre had been in the tunnels once in those 3 weeks. He determined the spots where the charges should be placed, marking each with a red spray-painted X.

Which was a damn dumb idea. Like we're the only ones down in the tunnels. Jesus, every kid over 15 has been down here. Somebody's gonna figure out what the X means.

Bill had a dozen other reasons for mistrusting Mr. X.

'Dammit now I'm doing it, the guy's name is Andre.'

It was Bill & Pete's job to get the explosives from Tongue Point to the tunnels and then hide them close to the Hotel.

Of course, Andre won't be involved. Like the bastard can't get his hands dirty. Can't do any actual labor.

The work on the tunnels and the whole People's Army thing consumed both Pete & Bill. They had no time for any side jobs. They needed money and Andre seemed to have it.

Andre spent a lot of time at the First Bank of Astoria across from the hotel. He almost seemed to work there. The night Andre went into the tunnels, he spent more time looking at the foundation of the bank than he did at the hotel.

Andre kept wining and dining Pete like they were going steady. Bill could have gone to these dinners, but the political rants went on way too long. There was to be some big payoff for Bill, Pete and to a lesser degree, Joe, after the bombing. Like a reward for starting the 'Revolution.'

Bill wasn't as hell-bent on starting a revolution as Pete. He needed walking around money right now. So, he went to Andre and pretty much demanded it. In the end, Andre gave him $100.

And that's another thing, almost all the bills are burnt. Some more than others. It's weird. Can I pay for stuff with burnt money?

The waitress finally got around to taking Bill's order.

"Double cheeseburger with bacon, fries, and chocolate malt. And a beer to start." It made Bill mad they always asked for his ID.

The burger was the first real meal Bill ate in a while. It made him feel better.

The tab came to $3.10. Bill laid a $10 bill on the counter.

"I can't take that." The waitress looked at it like the bill was on fire. "It's burnt."

"It's not burnt, just a little charred on one end. There's nothing wrong with it."

"I'm not taking it, give me some other money."

Bill took the other bills from his wallet, hoping to find one in better shape. The best-looking bill was already on the counter.

"Are you telling me all of the money you have is burnt?"

"Charred a little not burnt. My wallet dropped in a campfire." Even Bill didn't believe himself.

"Well, you'd better come up with something."

Jeff Steele sat at the counter having his lunch and reading the Oregonian. He worked at the First Bank of Astoria across the street and always had a tuna melt and coke for lunch. Always at the JJA Hotel, always at the counter, sitting on the same stool. The JJA had been going downhill for some time, but Jeff was a creature of habit. In a big way.

He couldn't help overhear the commotion at the end of the counter.

"I'll help the young man out. Here, give me your ten & I'll give you one a little newer," Jeff said.

Bill, his face bright red, exchanged the bill with the stranger, thanked him, paid his bill, and left a penny tip.

Jeff Steele finished his lunch and Coke, paid the tab and generous tip, and folded the newspaper under his arm. He stopped to talk to a couple of people he knew on the sidewalk.

When Jeff got to his desk, his first call was to the Oregon State Police and his second to the FBI in Portland. He reported burnt money being passed in Astoria.

37

December 20

"TIME TO GO," the deputy called out as he clanged his keys on the open cell door. Merri struggled awake from a deep sleep she had not experienced in days. Her bed was a simple pad thrown atop a metal frame. No pillow. But she was not complaining. The cell was warm, and she was safe.

Merri could have slept all day.

"My shift's over, and you need to disappear before someone else takes over."

Merri rubbed her eyes as she stood up. The deputy escorted her to the front of the precinct. A waist-high wall and gate separated the precinct's front and back sections. He took her arm gently as he opened the gate to usher her out. Merri recoiled from his grasp. It caught him off guard.

"Sorry," he apologized. She glared at him while exiting the building.

Merri wandered down the street, no direction in mind. A mother dressed in a collared, knee-length dress, pearl necklace, and white gloves guided her six-year-old son around Merri giving her a wide berth.

"Mommy, who's that woman?" the boy asked while pointing at the disheveled Merri.

"Never mind." She hurried him along to safety. "It is no one."

Merri stood on the corner of Salmon and Broadway, next to the entrance to the Portland Hilton. She just stood there. With no idea what to do.

"Honey, are you all right?"

The voice was soft and southern.

"What?"

"I asked if you were alright." The woman was tall, with high heels and a very short skirt. Smoking a Virginia Slim cigarette.

"Yeah, yeah, I, I'm good"

"You don't look it."

"Can I have a cigarette… please?" Merri hadn't smoked before she got to the shelter. Almost everyone there did. It helped her from feeling hungry and made her seem warmer.

The two women stood on the corner smoking. And somehow Merri's story came tumbling out.

All of it.

"And I just lost it, Lashelle. I've got to get a job, some money. Any ideas you can give me would help."

"Well, there is someone who'd help you. He's helped other girls. Works out of the east side. He has a nice house and girls stay there. He gets them clothes, shoes, a haircut. Kind of the whole makeover thing."

"It sounds good! How much does all that cost?"

"Oh, there'll be a price," Lashelle said.

A Portland PD cruiser gave out a short blast on the siren. Lashelle disappeared in an instant. Inside the cruiser were the two policemen from the night before.

Officer Hanson rolled down the driver's side window and said,

"If you stay in the jail tonight it'll be because I arrested you. This time the cell door will be locked."

"We were just talking," Merri stammered.

"Are you looking for more trouble?"

"No, sir, I'm not. She was saying she knew someone who could help me."

"You don't want that kind of help. Stay away from her."

Merri was hungry. She found a diner and entered. The red Naugahyde booths and stools were old and torn. A diamond-stamped stainless-steel wall held a glass display of the day's bakery goods. The Formica table tops were scratched, their off-yellow pattern worn away in spots.

Merri sat on a mushroom-shaped stool at the counter. The chrome-plating on its legs were peeling. It was off-peak. Many spots were open for guests to sit at. She watched the counter girl, a woman in her forty's, work the room delivering meals and coffee and slices of apple pie. The server passed by several times but never approached Merri. Merri tried to get her attention, but the woman never looked her way.

Merri reached into her pocket and pulled out a messy wad of bills. Her money was dwindling. The server approached.

"Listen," she said in a hushed tone, "The owner says I can't serve you. You understand, don't you, hon?"

Merri brushed her matted hair back away from her eyes.

"I'm not your 'hon' and I'm not leaving. I'm hungry. And I can pay."

"I saw that. It's not me. It's the guy cooking back there." Merri glanced at the fat, bald man behind the pass-through window. "You don't want me to lose my job, do you?"

Merri shook her head. "Sell me a piece of apple pie and I will leave."

"Promise?"

Merri nodded.

The server plated up a piece of apple pie and slid it into a small, brown paper sack.

"Be careful. Keep the bag sideways or you'll have a mess." Merri took the sack. She felt a ceramic plate inside. "I put a fork in there. They're cheap… like the owner." To avoid dirtying her starched apron, the server wiped her hands on a towel folded on the countertop. Merri held out two dollars to pay. The server looked around at her boss. His back was toward the pass-through window. "Keep it. Enjoy the pie."

Merri left searching for a safe place to eat her pie. Everyone's eyes stared at her. Or avoided her completely. She found herself at the park near Grace Gospel Mission. As she crossed the street, Cowboy Joe sat on 'his' bench. He looked the same. Same clothes. Same cowboy hat.

She recognized something in his shopping cart. Under the tarp, sticking out one corner, was her suitcase. Anger filled her. She stomped over to him, her face red.

"I want it back," she demanded.

"What?"

"You stole my suitcase from me. It's all I have. And I want it back."

"You accuse me of theft, then you want me to help you?"

"What I want is my suitcase. I'm not going to apologize to you, crazy man. You stole my suitcase. I want it back. Simple to understand, even for you."

"Now you insult me," Cowboy Joe said in a calm voice that started to disarm her.

"Please," she said without the energy to fight on. He waved his arm inviting her to sit next to him. She did. He looked into her eyes before he spoke.

"If you invited me to dinner at your home, I would be respectful. I would complement the food or say nothing at all. If we were Japanese, I would remove my shoes at the door."

"And what does that have to do with my suitcase?"

"This is my home. You are a guest in it. It would be wise to learn who I am before throwing around strong accusations. You don't know me – don't pretend that you do."

"My suitcase is right there," Merri declared.

Cowboy Joe took a deep breath.

"If you understood the street, you would know only Dopers steal, and they live on the south side of town. The rest of us have a code."

"That's not important. My case is. Please."

"It IS important if you end up living here."

"I don't want to live here."

"But you are. I see you every day."

Merri went silent. He was right. She was on the streets.

"And because of that, I saved your case knowing you would be around."

"Truly?"

"Have I yet to lie to you?"

She paused.

"All men lie. They eat lies for breakfast."

"I feel the pain in your comments."

"Yeah, well, that's my life."

"And that life has brought you here?"

"Yup."

"Not booze? Not dope?"

"No way."

"Then, take a walk with me."

"Why?"

"Humor me. Do you have a busy day scheduled?"

Cowboy Joe caught a brief smile. She stood, and he led the way.

"Wait. My suitcase."

"No one will touch it. The code. Remember?"

"But if you didn't steal my case, someone else did."

"Bengie. A doper. I made him give it back. Nothing in it of value anyway. We sent him south. He won't bother us up here anymore."

"I see."

Cowboy Joe led Merri to the other side of the park. Sitting against a tree trunk, a lost soul slept, his hand draped over a small paper bag twisted around the neck of the pint bottle of whiskey. They walked past. The man never moved. At the corner, another man stood, working the traffic as it stopped for a red light.

On a cardboard sign, he had scrawled 'Need parts 4 spaceship. Trying to get home. Anything helps.'

"Drinkers are more solitary," Cowboy Joe pointed out. "They choose booze over food. Sad."

Merri stopped and stared at the man she stood next to. *Who is he?*

"You talk down about these men. They're just another you."

"Not down. I don't talk down about them. I simply want you to understand what it's like on the streets. Who you are living among? What are they like?"

"I'm not planning on living here. Not permanently at least.

"Good to hear. Let me show you one more thing."

"You talk about Dopers and Alcoholics like you are different."

"Oh, different? Yes and no. We all share the streets, I guess, but when we get around the corner ahead, you'll understand better."

As they turned the corner, Merri looked down the street. It was lined by two and three-story brick buildings. All gray and brown and weathered. Cowboy Joe took her to a narrow, empty lot nestled between two buildings. Empty in that there was no building on it but filled with homeless lean-tos built of wood pallets and tarps and large cardboard boxes. There was more order to it than the pictures of homeless camps she had seen. On the right brick wall, a mural covered it from street to back corner. In bright, hopeful colors, it depicted people standing in a valley with the sun rising over the surrounding hills.

"The people living here do so without fear of being kicked off the land or harassed by the cops."

"What about the landowner?"

"He supports it."

"Really?"

"He feels the people living here deserve the use of the place."

"Impressive. I would think he would worry about the land's value."

"One man's trash is another man's treasure."

"I guess."

"There are no dopers or alcoholics living here. They have places to help them if they seek it. The people here choose to be, or circumstances overwhelmed them. What could be a better use of the land?"

"Hmmm. I love the mural. It is beautiful."

"Thank you."

"Did I compliment you?"

"Yes."

"You painted that? It's fantastic. What talent. Why not do it for a living? You'd be rich."

"And then?" Joe questioned.

"Then you would not have to live on the street anymore." Cowboy Joe lowered his head. "I'm sorry. That was thoughtless of me."

"No. No. I was thinking." Joe replied. "We are talking about me when we need to be talking about you. Say, are you hungry?"

"Famished."

"Come on. We're having lunch. I know just the spot."

Merri looked confused. Cowboy Joe slept in a shelter every night. Spent his days on a park bench.

I was right from the start. He's crazy. Taking me for a fool. It's not his mural. Now he wants to take me back to the shelter and 'buy' me lunch.

"Joe. You don't have to buy me lunch," she said giving him an out. "Let's go get my suitcase and I'll be on my way."

"No, I insist." He walked with a confident pace Merri had not noticed before.

The couple walked two blocks before Cowboy Joe stopped, pulled open a heavily-sculpted wood door with brass trimmings and lead glass inserts. Merri sensed it was a high-end dinner house.

"Joe, I don't think—"

"Come on. Don't be shy."

They passed by the lounge. The bartender, busy polishing glasses, took the time to acknowledge them.

"Hi, Joe," he said.

Merri was startled. "Did he just—"

Cowboy Joe kept walking, entering the dining room. Though daylight outside, it was dark. Rich stained woods and brass railings decorated the room. Plush red high-back booths made for intimate dining. Joe kept walking. Between the dining room and the kitchen, separated by wood and lead glass walls, a single half-round booth matching those in the main room, awaited them. Cowboy Joe motioned her to sit. He hung his hat on a brass hook and slid into the booth.

Her jaw was open. It was hard to comprehend. She would not have believed it, but the bartender knew him by name.

"What is going on?"

Cowboy Joe smiled.

"Great restaurants recognize their best customers."

"That's not what I mean, and you know it. Cough up."

Just then, Evelyn, a matronly server, approached the table. She had been with the restaurant for fourteen years, and if she was working, she took care of Joe.

"May I offer you a cocktail," she asked looking at Merri. "Joe is having a Macallan's neat."

"I'll have a martini. Shaken." Merri had seen *You Only Live Twice* at the Job Corps and ordered as if she was James Bond.

"Will Beefeater's be all right?" Evelyn asked.

Merri had no idea what Evelyn was talking about but answered yes anyway.

"Very well. I will return shortly."

Evelyn whisked away.

Merri, still in awe, confronted Joe.

"I am overwhelmed by this place and by you. You owe me an explanation."

"I do. First, do you acknowledge you misjudged me? Who I am? That I stole your suitcase?"

"Guilty as charged. I am sorry."

"Not another word about it. I choose to be on the street. You, my dear, did not make that choice. Am I right?"

"Right."

"I used to live on our estate with my mother." Joe's voice softened. "But I have been fighting a mental disorder. They haven't given it a name yet. I have fits at times. It scares my mother and she put a restraining order on me. I'm not allowed within a thousand yards of her."

"How could she do that to her son?"

"It is best for her tranquility. She's been on tranquilizers for twenty years now. Who knows how my issue will progress? It might be a smart move.

"Anyway, I never fit in with the elite crowd. I sometimes embarrassed Mom. Now I choose a simpler life and I embarrass her all the time."

Evelyn approached with the cocktails.

"We'll order in a minute, Evelyn."

She nodded and left silently.

"What about the halfway house?"

"Part of my mother's foundation. They humor me there."

"And the lot for the homeless?"

"Mine."

"And the mural?"

"Mine and the building I used as a canvas."

"Seriously? Wow."

"We came here to talk about you, remember? What happened?"

Merri explained her expulsion from the Job Corps making sure to blame Tom, Scott, and Larry for her demise. Cowboy Joe was attentive but not buying her story. At least not how she viewed the events.

Evelyn returned, and Joe ordered lunch for them both.

As their meal progressed, Cowboy Joe delved deeper into Merri's past. Her pain. Her father. Her mistrust of men. How they always let her down. He felt for her but saw a flaw in how she dealt with challenges in her life. Before he could approach the subject, Evelyn returned.

"Can I suggest a strawberry tiramisu? Chocolate Mousse?"

Merri remembered the apple pie she had purchased earlier.

"My pie? What happened to my apple pie? I had it with me when I was discussing... okay, yelling at you about my suitcase."

"You set it on the bench as we 'discussed' things."

"The chef makes a great apple pie," Evelyn noted. "Good as my mother's, but don't tell her that."

"If he has a piece," Joe said, "we'll take it to go."

"Yes, sir."

Evelyn returned with a to-go box as Joe had requested. She disappeared into the background but was attentive to the table. The bill and a healthy tip were put on Joe's tab. He paid once a month.

"Well, I guess it's time to go," Merri said with a disappointing sound in her voice. "Thank you for your hospitality, Joe, which I don't deserve. I am, however, glad to have met you."

"We're not done yet, my dear."

"Oh?"

"Remember when you agreed that you misjudged me?"

"Yes."

"Much of life is perception and how we react. The mind is like a parachute." He paused. "It only works when open.

"Tom might have been flirting with that other woman. Maybe not. You, however, never took the time to seek the truth. Whose fault is that? And Scott? All he did was buy an attractive woman a drink. You chose to drink it. You knew the Job Corps rules. A skydiver learns to always pack his own chute. Only he then has responsibility for what happens when he pulls the cord.

"Control your own destiny, Merri." Cowboy Joe grabbed the single piece of pie and handed it to her.

"This building is a hotel. Go to the front desk and check-in. One night only. Take the pie and think about what we discussed. You don't belong on the streets, Merri."

"I cannot accept, Joe. This is too much."

"As you've seen, I can afford it. Now go enjoy your pie."

Her view of Cowboy Joe changed drastically that day. So did her outlook on life.

Joe stayed behind a minute. He watched as she talked to the man behind the front desk. Satisfied he had touched her life, Cowboy Joe stood up and walked to the door. As he passed Merri, he caught her attention.

"Pack your own chute, Merri."

Merri scraped her fork across the paper plate catching every bit of the apple pie. As she savored the final bite, her eyes closed, and she allowed herself to fall back on the bed. Soft. Pampering. She fell asleep.

Rap. Rap.

The bellhop knocked on Merri's door. As she opened it, the porter held out her suitcase.

"Joe?" she half stated, and half questioned.

The porter smiled, nodded, and left. Merri tossed the case on the bed and headed for the restroom.

Merri immersed herself in a hot shower. As the water washed away a week of dirt, Merri contemplated what Cowboy Joe had said. He got everything right but one. She towel-dried her hair as she rushed back to the bed. She threw open the case and reached inside.

Cowboy Joe was right. Nothing inside the suitcase had value... for Bengie, the doper. But for Merri, it held everything.

She opened an envelope and held up a ticket back to Astoria the Job Corps administrator had given her.

Suddenly she realized what truly mattered in her world.

38

THE UNRELENTING RAIN soaked Andre as he exited his car and retrieved his tool bag from the trunk. He crossed the street to the tunnels below Astoria. The wind howled and the chilled ocean air bit his skin. *This dreary-ass place* he mumbled.

Andre's muttonchops dripped water as he peered between the cement supports at the entrance to the tunnels. The floors in this area of the underground were sand which made walking laborious for the lazy Andre. The cement ceilings in the area were low hung. Everything radiated coldness. He would have delegated this shit to someone else but that would mean bringing him in on the job. He had split too many jobs and ended with only piss money. Not this time. This would be his big score.

He had been here once before with the People's Army guys. *What a joke.* They showed Andre where they would stash the C-4 before he positioned them, and he analyzed the support structure for the hotel they wanted to blow.

His real goal was the First Bank of Astoria across the street on the corner of 14th and Duane. When built in the twenties, the bank was a modern marvel. The stately main floor featured large paned glass windows, polished granite floors, teller cages with etched glass and wrought iron façade. Sculpted wood banisters led to mezzanine offices. The focal point of the main floor was a grand staircase leading down to the deposit box section and the bank's main vault.

Andre used his Delco flashlight through the tunnels, its light bouncing off cement beams and walls. At Fourteenth and Commercial Streets, he stopped. He stood directly below the entrance to the First Bank of Astoria. Andre stared at the tunnel wall in front of him. It was the only thing standing between him and the bank's main vault; the source of his new fortune.

It was Thursday evening. Tomorrow it would go down. Today, he would plant the explosives strategically around the bank vault wall and the hotel but wait to attach the detonators until right before the event. Less possibility of being discovered by a chance wanderer.

The plan was good. Andre saw it in his mind's eye. Two blocks from the hotel, Andre would push the plunger sending a radio signal to the detonators in the C-4. Then all hell would break loose.

He had found an ambulance in a junkyard in Portland, paid cash for it, and parked it three blocks from the bank. As chaos ensued, Andre, dressed as an ambulance driver, would head into the tunnels to the blown bank wall. *No one will question me. I'm brilliant.*

He would throw the money into a body bag and carry it to the truck. Nothing would look out of place. He did, however, need a second guy to carry out the "body" with him. He found his accomplice on the river's edge living among the brush and arching trees. The homeless man was excited about his payment: a case of vodka. Andre hadn't decided if he would trust the man after the job or not. If not, he would simply bludgeon him and leave him among the rubble of the hotel.

Satisfaction filled his thoughts.

As he came back to reality, he walked to where the guys had stashed the C-4 in the tunnels. He told them what he needed to do today was dangerous work and it was best he worked alone. The guys were fine with that.

There, in an always-dark corner, Andre found the cases with an old brown bedspread draped over them. *Perfect.* He looked around, saw no one, and tossed the spread aside. He lifted the first block in a smooth sweep and headed for the hotel. There, he attached the C-4 to the dark, unseen side of the hotel posts. It took Andre forty-five minutes to finish that part of the job.

Next, Andre carried a M112 of C-4 to the bank. All he needed here was a door-sized hole to enter the vault, but he needed to be careful. Too little C-4 and he would not get into the vault. Too much and Andre would blow up the money.

Andre turned. Felt a presence. Movement. No one there. Shrugging his shoulders, he wrote it off to nerves.

In the damp, chilling atmosphere of the tunnels, Andre attached the final C-4 to the bank wall. He stepped back analyzing his accomplishment. Was there a detail forgotten? He had one chance at this. Andre retraced his steps to the John Jacob Astor Hotel, deep in thought. He missed a shadowy figure approaching from the rear.

"What's going on?"

"Jesus!" Andre yelled. His spine shivered. His mind processed his worse fears. He was found out. All his work for nothing. But as Andre turned, he recognized a friendly face. Bill.

Bill looked up the cement hotel wall and the C-4 attached to its dark crevices.

"Looks good. You've been hard at work."

Andre was unsure how much Bill had seen. Adrenaline raced through Mr. X's blood.

"God damn, Bill. You about gave me a heart attack."

Bill said nothing. Andre could not read him. Bill saw the two M112s were gone.

"Used all the C-4, did you?" Bill pointed to an empty wrapper with his toe.

Andre hesitated. *Did he know something? Was he setting him up?*

"It's a big structure. Takes a lot to bring it down. But we will tomorrow." He looked up at his work sure of his declaration.

"What about the bank?" Bill had seen Andre set C-4 next to the bank wall on the other side of the street.

"Well... I want to bring down the street structure between the buildings to be sure the hotel is razed, and our mission fulfilled." That sounded good to Andre. He hoped it satisfied Bill.

"Why don't you take me over to the bank?" Bill walked through the tunnel to the bank wall. Andre followed, anger building, wary of Bill's interest in his work.

The explosives at the bank were placed differently than for the hotel. Lower. Not as much of it. Bill's instincts kicked in. He knew from years of being in the tunnels that on the other side of the wall was the bank's vault. "Seems odd, Andre." Bill never liked the man. "If you want to weaken the street structure, why no C-4 on the street side?"

"It's held up by the wall you are looking at." *Was Bill suspicious?* Andre wanted no loose ends. "Take down the wall and you take down the street."

"Are you done?"

"Yes."

"The guys need to see this, Andre. Something smells."

"What do you mean?" Andre knew Bill was going to create problems for him. Perhaps blow the whole gig. *Unacceptable.*

Bill turned away from Andre to face the bank again. "This wall. The guys need to see what you've been doing. I don't like it."

"And I don't like people who second-guess my plans." Andre had retrieved a hammer from his bag and swung it as hard as he could at Bill's skull. The concussion sent Bill slamming into the wall. He dropped to the sand. Bill started to reach up for help, but life ebbed from him first.

Andre wiped off his hammer on Bill's shirt. Stuck it in Bill's belt.

No feeling of remorse.

Grabbing Bill at his armpits, Andre pulled him to a nearby cement rail wall meant to keep a rising tide from advancing. He laid Bill on the rail's top and grabbed his hammer before pushing him over. *No one will find him for days. I'll be long gone by then. Let the crabs have a feast.*

He had finished his work… for the People's Army. He smiled. *The Army of Idiots.*

39

December 21

THE KNOCK ON TOM'S DOOR broke his slumber. On the other side of the door was Fred, a casual friend at Job Corps.

"Hey, Tom. Sorry. Had no way of knowing you were taking a nap. It's the weekend, but it's afternoon already."

"No problem. What's up?"

"I was at the office in the lobby waiting for Larry. When he came in, the receptionist told him she got a call last night. Merri. She's coming back."

"Incredible. When?"

"That's all I know, man."

"I've got to see Larry. Thanks, Fred."

"Good luck."

"Yeah, man."

Tom entered the Job Corps lobby, his shirt buttons not matching their holes and his hair only hand-combed.

The receptionist looked at the disheveled young man. "Hi, Tom. The winter solstice is today. The shortest day of the year. I guess it makes getting up hard."

Tom ran a hand through his hair.

"I need to talk to Larry. Now. Is he in?"

"He is. I'll let him know you are here." She started to call him on her Teledex machine, but Tom barged into Larry's office.

"Good afternoon, Tom. You're energetic today."

"We need to talk, sir."

"It would be better if you allowed my receptionist to announce you… as you've been taught."

"I understand, sir. But this is important."

"So is protocol—"

"Okay. You're right. I apologize."

"Accepted. Now, what is so urgent?"

"I hear Merri is coming back to the Corp?"

"Good news travels fast. She will have an interview with the board. See if she is ready to return. It's possible. That's all I can say."

"Come on, Larry. You know the score. I haven't seen her forever. I miss her. How is she? She okay?"

"I am not at liberty to say."

Tom looked at him frustrated.

"Look. I know you like this girl, Tom. I do too. She is coming this afternoon from Portland. Meeting with us tomorrow. We'll go from there."

"Wait. What did you say? She's coming into town this afternoon? On the bus?"

"Yes. Why? Are you thinking of meeting her? You might be too late. She's coming in on the 5:20 it says here."

Tom glanced at the clock on the wall. Five to five. *I'll never make it in time taking the bus. And the station is part of the John Jacob Astor Hotel! The guys will blow it up as Merri is arriving.*

"Larry. I need your help. Merri and everyone on that bus is in grave danger. I need to get to the bus station. Now."

"What are you talking about?"

"No time for details. Call the depot. Please. Is the bus on time?"

"But, Tom."

"Trust me." Tom looked into Larry's eyes. Larry knew he was serious. He found the depot's number in the phone book and confirmed the buses' arrival.

"It's on time, Tom."

"I have to go."

Larry reached in his pocket and tossed Tom his car keys. "Have more respect for my car than you have for me."

Tom smiled, amazed. "Not possible, sir."

40

December 21

ANDRE HURRIED INTO THE TUNNEL ENTRANCE. Practically ran to the charges he had placed around John Jacob Astor Hotel. Out of breath. Tension sky high, Andre thought of what was about to happen... his big score. All of it planned and executed by him. He didn't need anyone. This would prove it. As soon as he set off the detonators at the hotel and next at the bank, it would all start. No turning back.

Andre's hand shook as he stuck the first detonator into the clay-like C-4 under the hotel. At the request of the People's Army idiots, he would set off the C-4 at 5:21 pm., the exact time of the summer solstice. He would push the plunger activating the detonators. Andre checked his watch.

Seven minutes from now.

COUNTDOWN: 7:00 minutes

Larry called ahead to the guard gate. As Larry's beat-up Ford Falcon approached, the guard raised the rail to let him pass. Tom never slowed down. Shocks bottomed out as he took the speed bump full throttle. The guard scratched his head, a million questions he'd have to ask Larry about later.

Winding past the old Naval shipyard, the road from Job Corps led up the hill to Leif Erickson Boulevard eating away time. At the intersection, Tom looked both ways for the Greyhound bus carrying his Merri. It was ahead of him on its way downtown. *I've got to catch the bus before it gets to the hotel.*

Shit.

He pulled out in front of an old truck causing the driver to brake. It was the least of Tom's worries. He sped up pulling behind the bus. *Now what?*

He honked. Honked again.

A couple people sitting in the buses' last row looked around. The bus kept going.

Shit.

Tom had no other choice. He rode the center line looking to pass the Greyhound. A logging truck bore down on him from the oncoming lane and he returned to safety behind the bus.

He was burning time.

Shit.

As the logging truck passed, he moved over the center line again. The road took an arching left turn near 39th Street.

Two cars approached. He was forced to wait until they passed. Tom checked his watch. The bus would arrive just as the hotel blew up.

Shit.

COUNTDOWN: 6:08 minutes

"Where's Bill?" Peter asked as he looked at Bill's mattress on the floor.

"Didn't come home last night," Joe said.

Peter shook his head. "Should be here. This is big. He should be here, damn it."

The two remaining members of the People's Army stumbled outside their basement squat. They had the perfect vantage point, a view of downtown, the river, and the John Jacob Astor Hotel.

Still no Bill.

COUNTDOWN: 5:54 minutes

Andre didn't bother to check that no one had disturbed the site where he had left Bill's body. After he killed him, Andre hadn't given Bill Nikula another thought. He ran through the tunnel under Fourteenth Street and set the detonator into the C-4 at the bank vault wall.

COUNTDOWN: 5:17 minutes

One hand on the horn, the other with a death grip on the steering wheel, Tom pushed the gas pedal to the floor and turned into the oncoming lane. An approaching car swerved viciously right to avoid Tom and went through the front window of Home Bakery.

The Falcon came even to the bus driver's window. Tom honked. Honked again. The driver looked at him but shook his head at the crazy driver. A Dodge pickup truck was approaching Tom. He needed to drop back out of its way or…

Tom gave the Falcon all it had. He gained on the bus. Tom swerved in front. The bus clipped Larry's car and it spun around. The bus driver hit his brakes, the bus coming to a stop inches from Larry's Falcon.

COUNTDOWN: 3:22 minutes

Peter and Joe gazed over downtown Astoria, its homes, and the hotel.

"Too bad," Joe said, "Bill isn't here to see this."

"He should be here, damn it," Peter barked.

"Hope he at least got laid."

"Joe, life is a series of priorities."

"For Bill," Joe said, "it's getting laid."

Peter shook his head and checked his watch.

Still no Bill.

COUNTDOWN: 3:03 minutes

Tom ran to the bus door, banging on it. The terrified bus driver refused to let him in. Tom yelled, "Don't go to the depot right now. It's dangerous," Tom said. "I know. I sound crazy."

The driver nodded. He was crazy all right. But he might be telling the truth.

The bus doors opened. Tom rushed past the driver and frightened passengers looking for Merri. He found her near the back. She stood. Confused. Amazed. Happy to see Tom.

Tom ran down the aisle and Merri was in his arms again.

COUNTDOWN: 2:18 minutes

The bus filled with flashing red light. Sirens wailed.

An Astoria police car shot past the bus. Before Tom and Merri could assimilate things, three black on black FBI Dodge Monacos flew by.

"My god," Tom said.

"What?"

"Merri, no time to explain. Do not go to the station. Please. Stay here. I promise. I'll be back."

"But I—"

"I promise."

She watched Tom leave. Going into danger. She did not understand but trusted him.

COUNTDOWN: 1:48 minutes

Tom ran down the street toward the John Jacob Astor Hotel.

It's too late.

Astoria police and county sheriff cars were already there. Five FBI Monacos arrived circling to predetermined locations.

They're going to die. Gotta stop them.

Tom ran to an officer standing next to his vehicle talking on his radio.

"Sir, get everyone out of the hotel. Now. It's going to explode."

The officer turned.

"And how would you know?"

"I'll explain later, sir. But we don't have time. Please."

"You have a lot of explaining to do. Right now."

COUNTDOWN: 0:38 seconds

Tom ignored the officer and ran past him.

"The hotel is going to blow!" Tom yelled at anyone whose attention he could get.

"Hey, you! Stop. Turn around," the officer demanded. He caught up to Tom, huffing; his too many doughnuts at Home Bakery slowing him down. "Step back. I have a couple questions for you." The officer grabbed Tom's arm and led him back away from the hotel.

"But we—"

"Don't move. Stay right here. You can tell your story to the FBI. He's coming over here right now."

"But—" Tom glanced down Commercial and noticed Andre's GTO parked in front of Loop Jacobsen Jewelers.

Oh, shit.

Tom ignored the officer. He ran across the intersection to Loop Jacobsen's and stood at the door. He could hear someone inside. With trepidation, Tom put his key in the lock and eased the door open. He squeezed through the gap without ringing the bell that set on top of the door.

The curtain that separated the workshop from the rest of the store was closed. He parted the curtain. Hunched in front of the store's safe knelt Andre working on the hinges with an acetylene torch.

The asshole is going through with his fallback plan!

Tom moved into the workshop space. Between Tom and Andre was a jumble of tools and a burlap sack. Mixed in with the tools, Tom saw a gun. He bent down, picked it up and using both hands, aimed the gun at Andre.

"WHAT IN THE HELL DO YOU THINK YOU'RE DOING?"

Intent on his work, with a welding mask on and the sound of the torch, Andre hadn't heard or noticed anything behind him. Tom's shout almost caused him to drop the torch. Andre turned to confront Tom. He looked him in the eyes. The gun shook in Tom's hands. Andre turned the flame up on the torch, stood up and waved it at Tom.

"You won't use the gun, Tom. You're crapping your pants just thinking about it. I've stared down a gun before. I've killed before. Your boy Bill? You can find him across the street behind a chair wall. Dead. You don't have the..."

Tom pulled the trigger.

"Jeesus, you shot me . . . I'm hit . . . I'm hit."

Tom shot him again.

"Stop . . . stop . . . don't kill me. My arm's burning!"

"I was aiming for your head. Shut up or I'll shoot you again."

COUNTDOWN: 0:00

Peter and Joe sat on the hillside waiting for the hotel to go down. It did not. They waited. Nothing. Peter hit Joe on the arm.

"What's going on?"

"I don't know."

"Damn it," Peter said. "I was a fool to get Andre involved in our plan to blow up the hotel. We are the People's Army. Not him."

Peter stood staring at the hotel. Its failure to blow. His failure.

"Thank you for standing," a dark-suited man said behind Peter. He grabbed Peter's arms slapping cold metal cuffs around both wrists.

"You have the right to remain silent. Anything you say will be used against you in a court of law; you have the right to consult with an attorney and to have that attorney present during questioning, and, if you are indigent, an attorney will be provided at no cost to represent you. Do you understand these rights?"

Peter looked at the man. Begrudgingly, he said, "Yes."

"Good."

A second FBI agent cuffed Joe. He pulled a card from his jacket pocket and read Joe his rights. This was new for the agents. Only three years earlier, the Supreme Court found Ernesto Arturo Miranda's Fifth and Sixth Amendment rights had been violated.

"What's the charge?" Joe asked.

"Oh, I believe we have a lot on you two. We heard Peter here confess moments ago. Don't plan on going on any trips soon, men. Except for the one to prison." He smiled at his partner as they led Peter and Joe to their waiting car.

"Get in boys, watch your heads and I'll explain conspiracy to you."

PART EIGHT
Wind with Rain

41

TOM'S CALL TO THE FBI made the difference. They had been following the trail of burnt money up the coast and, with his call, they had tied it to the People's Army and Andre Demico.

The FBI coordinated with the Astoria PD & Fire, Clatsop County Sheriff, and the Oregon State Patrol. The agencies worked well together on the biggest operation to hit Clatsop County in decades.

They evacuated the John Jacob Astor Hotel first. Then buildings within a five-block area. All downtown streets blocked, and ferry service halted.

An FBI agent had watched in the darkness of the tunnels as Andre set the detonators under the hotel and bank. He let him escape knowing other agents awaited Andre at the ambulance. The agent walked to the two C-4 sites and removed their detonators.

Unseen by the FBI agent, Andre headed down a different tunnel away from the ambulance and the other agents waiting for him. His real destination: Loop Jacobsen Jewelers and his GTO getaway.

Andre's accomplice, the homeless man from 8th Street, was turned over to local authorities. He would be processed and released.

The trials for Joe, Peter and Tom went quickly. The grand jury did not indict Tom, ruling his actions self-defense. The acetylene torch being used as a weapon.

Joe and Peter got 24 months state prison time, plus 5 years probation. Their lawyer said, "If being stupid was a crime, they could have got life."

Andre's trial took longer. After his wounds healed, he was indicted for conspiracy (attempted bombing of the John Jacob Astor Hotel,) murder (he confessed to killing Bill,) attempted murder (using the welding torch as the weapon); breaking and entering, and attempted robbery.

Andre was found guilty on all charges.

Then the Feds got involved. He was charged in federal court with the bank robbery in San Jose and Cottage Grove, the attempted First Bank of Astoria robbery, and the murder of Leonard Henderson.

Again, Andre found guilty on all counts. On the fourth year of his federal time, a cellmate stabbed Andre to death with a Bic pen.

42

FRANK VAN WINKLE was placing the jewelry from the new safe in the display cases and storefront windows. As he set the rose-pink ring box in the window, he had an idea.

"Hey, Dad. Tom asked us to hold his wages, right?"

"Of course. He wants the money put towards the ring."

"Exactly. And he single-handedly saved our you-know-what during the burglary, right?"

"Right. And?"

"And I'm thinking we need to reward him and get the young couple off to a good start."

"What do you mean?"

"I mean, they're great together, and he's worked hard here. Why don't we waive the remaining balance he owes… as a wedding gift?"

"Waive the balance? Give it to him? This is why I'm in charge of finances."

"Dad, have a heart."

"I have a heart, son, and a head. But you're right. Let's give them the ring."